원미동 시인

도서출판 아시아에서는 《바이링궐 에디션 한국 현대 소설》을 기획하여 한국의 우수한 문학을 주제별로 엄선해 국내외 독자들에게 소개합니다. 이 기획은 국내외 우수한 번역가들이 참여하여 원작의 품격을 최대한 살렸습니다. 문학을 통해 아시아의 정체성과 가치를 살피는 데 주력해 온 도서출판 아시아는 한국인의 삶을 넓고 깊게 이해하는 데 이 기획이 기여하기를 기대합니다.

Asia Publishers present some of the very best modern Korean literature to readers worldwide through its new Korean literature series 〈Bi-lingual Edition Modern Korean Literature〉. We are proud and happy to offer it in the most authoritative translation by renowned translators of Korean literature. We hope that this series helps to build solid bridges between citizens of the world and Koreans through rich in-depth understanding of Korea.

바이링궐 에디션 한국 현대 소설 010

Bi-lingual Edition Modern Korean Literature 010

The Poet of Wŏnmi-dong

양귀자

원미동 시인

Yang Kwi-ja

ASIA
PUBLISHERS

Contents

원미동 시인 007
The Poet of Wŏnmi-dong

해설 081
Afterword

비평의 목소리 093
Critical Acclaim

작가 소개 100
About the Author

원미동 시인

The Poet of Wŏnmi-dong

남들은 나를 일곱 살짜리로서 부족함이 없는 그저 그만한 계집아이 정도로 여기고 있는 게 틀림없지만, 나는 결코 그저 그만한 어린아이는 아니다. 세상 돌아가는 이치를 다 알고 있다, 라고 말하는 게 건방지다면 하다못해 집안 돌아가는 사정이나 동네 사람들의 속마음 정도는 두루 알아맞힐 수 있는 눈치만큼은 환하니까. 그도 그럴 것이 사실을 말하자면 내 나이는 여덟 살이거나 아홉 살, 둘 중의 하나이다.

낳아 놓으니까 어찌나 부실한지 살아날 것 같지 않아 차일피일 출생신고를 미루다 보니 그렇게 된 것이라고 하는데 그나마 일곱 살짜리로 호적에 올려놓은 것만도 다행

I'm certain that people think of me as an ordinary seven-year-old girl, but I'm anything but an average child of the age. Let me just say that I know how the cookie crumbles. If it's too cocky for me to say, then I'll rephrase it: at least, I've got wits quick enough to sum up exactly what goes on in the minds of not only my family but the members of my town as well. Nothing really extraordinary, if you ask me, since I know my real age is either eight or nine, but definitely not seven.

I've been told that the registration of my birth was delayed, because I was so weak a baby that no one expected me to survive. Perhaps I should be thank-

인 셈이었다. 살아나기를 원하지 않았을 엄마 마음쯤은 나도 이미 알고 있는 터였다. 아버지는 좀 덜하지만 엄마는 나만 보면 늘상 으르렁거렸다. 꿈도 꾸지 않았던 자식이었지만 행여 해서 낳아 봤더니 원수 같은 또 딸이더라는 원성은 요사이도 노상 두고 하는 입버릇이니까 서운할 것도 없었다.

그것은 뭐 내가 일찌감치 철이 들어서가 아니라, 우리 집 사정이 워낙 그러했다. 내가 태어나던 해에 벌써 스물이 넘어 처녀티가 꽉 밴 큰언니에서 중학교 졸업반이던 막내 언니까지 딸이 무려 넷이었다. 마흔셋에 임신인지도 모르고 네댓 달 배를 키우다가 엄마는 여기저기 용하다는 점쟁이들한테 다녀 보고는 마침내 낳을 결심을 했었다는 것이다. 모든 점쟁이들이 '만장일치'로 아들이라고 주장해서였다. 그런 판에 또 조개 달고 나오기가 무렴해서였는지 냉큼 쑥 빠져나오지 못하고 버그적거리는 통에 산모를 반주검시켜 놓았다니 나로서는 입이 열 개라도 할 말이 없는 형편이었다. 그렇지만 실제로는 여덟 살이다, 아홉 살이다 자꾸 이랬다저랬다 하는 엄마도 과히 잘한 것은 없다. 내가 뭐 뺄셈 덧셈에 아주 까막눈인 줄 알지만 천만에, 우리 엄마는 내가 세 살이 될 때까지도 혹시 죽어

ful to my parents for entering my name in the family register at all as their seven-year-old child. I've already figured out that my mother didn't want me to survive. My father has not been quite as bad, but my mother has always been irritated with the mere sight of me. I still hear my mother habitually lamenting over her bad luck: although she'd never even dreamed of having the fifth child, she decided to have it, when she realized she was pregnant, hoping against hope, only to face the bitter reality of the fifth daughter. Now, I'm so used to her lamentation I don't even resent her.

It's not because I've already come of age prematurely, but because I can see clearly what's been going on in my family. When I was born, there were already four girls in the family, starting from my eldest sister, already over twenty and in the bloom of maidenhood, down to my youngest sister about to graduate from junior-high. At the age of forty-three, my mother didn't even realize she was pregnant until four or five months into it. She consulted as many gifted fortunetellers as possible, before she decided to have me. All of them assured her that it was a boy. To top it all, I half killed my mother by taking a long time to come out of her

주지나 않을까 기다린 게 분명하다.

내가 얼마나 구박덩이에 미운 오리 새끼인가를 길게 설명하고 싶지는 않다. 진짜 하고 싶은 이야기는 그런 따위 너절한 게 아니라 원미동 시인에 관한 것이니까. 내가 여러 가지 것을 많이 알고 있다고는 해도 솔직히 시가 뭣인지를 정확히 설명할 수는 없다. 얼추 짐작하기로 그것은 달 밝은 밤이나 파도가 출렁이는 바닷가에서 눈을 착 내리깔고 멋진 말을 몇 마디 내뱉는 것이 아닐까 여기지만 원미동 시인이 하는 것을 보면 매양 그렇지도 않은 모양이었다. 우리 동네에는 원미동 시인 말고도 원미동 카수니 원미동 멋쟁이, 원미동 똑똑이 등이 있다. 행복사진관 엄 씨 아저씨가 원미동 카수인데 지난번 '전국노래자랑' 부천 대회에서 예선에도 못 들고 떨어졌다니 대단한 솜씨는 못될 것이었다. 소라 엄마가 원미동 멋쟁이라는 것은 내가 가장 잘 안다. 그 보라색 매니큐어와 노랑머리는 소라 엄마뿐이니까. 원미동 똑똑이는, 부끄럽지만 우리 엄마다. 부끄럽다는 것은 남의 일에 간섭이 심하고 걸핏하면 싸움질이나 해대는 똑똑이는 욕이나 마찬가지라는 것을 알기 때문이다.

원미동 시인에게는 또 다른 별명이 있다. 퀭한 두 눈에

womb, perhaps feeling ashamed to come out with female genitals. I feel quite bad about it myself. Nevertheless, I don't think my mother's saying my real age is eight at some times and nine at others is exactly the epitome of good conduct either. She thinks I'm not good at adding and subtracting, but she's very much mistaken! Without a doubt, she must have wanted me to die, even when I became three.

I don't feel like going into details about the mistreatment I've been getting as the ugly duckling of my family. What I really want to talk about is not that kind of trivialities, but a poet living in Wŏnmi-dong, the town my family lives in. Though I know a lot of things, I can't honestly say that I know exactly what poetry is. I roughly guess it to be something like uttering some fancy words, with eyes downcast, either under a bright moon or on a surf-breaking beach. But then, judging from what Wŏnmi-dong poet does, it may not be all there is to poetry. Besides the poet, there are Wŏnmi-dong singer, Wŏnmi-dong smart dresser, and Wŏnmi-dong brain, etc. The town's singer is Mr. Om, who owns Happy Photo Studio. Despite his reputation, he didn't even make the preliminary round in the last Puch'ŏn con-

부스스한 머리칼, 사시사철 껴입고 다니는 물든 군용 점퍼와 희끄무레하게 닳아빠진 낡은 청바지가 밤중에 보면 꼭 몽달귀신 같다고 서울미용실의 미용사 경자 언니가 맨 처음 그를 '몽달씨'라고 부르기 시작했다. 경자 언니뿐만 아니라 우리 동네 사람이라면 누구나 그를 좀 경멸하듯이, 어린애 다루 듯 함부로 하는 게 보통인데 까닭은 그가 약간 돌았기 때문이라는 것이었다. 언제부터 어떻게 살짝 돌았는지는 모르지만 아무튼 보통 사람과 다른 것만은 틀림없었다. 몽달씨는 무궁화연립주택 삼 층에 살고 있었다. 베란다에 화분이 유난히 많고 새장이 세 개나 걸려 있는 몽달씨네 집은 여름이면 우리 동네에서는 드물게 윙윙거리며 하루 종일 에어컨이 돌아가는 부자였다. 시내에서 한약방을 하는 노인이 늘그막에 젊은 마누라를 얻어 아기자기하게 살아 보는 판인데 결혼한 제 형 집에 있지 않고 새살림 재미에 폭 빠진 아버지 곁으로 옮겨 온 막둥이였다. 그것부터가 팔불출이 짓이라고 강남부동산의 고흥댁 아줌마가 욕을 해쌌는데, 아들이 아버지와 함께 사는 게 왜 바보짓이라는 건지 알 수가 없었다.

그런 몽달씨에게 친구가 있다면 아마 내가 유일할 것이었다. 몽달씨 나이가 스물일곱이라니까 나보다 스무 살이

test, let alone the national one, so I figure he can't be that good. I admit, though, So-ra's mother is the town's smart dresser worthy of the name. She is the only one in town with purple nail polish and hair dyed yellow. I am ashamed to say that my mother is the town's brain, because I know people call my mother the nickname not to praise her but to ridicule her—a brain who's always poking her nose into others' affairs and picking quarrels with them.

Unlike the other celebrities of Wŏnmi-dong, the poet has another nickname. Sis Kyŏng-ja, a hairdresser at Seoul Beauty Salon, is the first person to call him Mr. Mongdal. According to her, the poet's hollow eyes, disheveled hair, dyed army jumper that he wears all year round, and worn-out jeans make him look, at night, like mongdal kwishin, the ghost of a man who dies before he ever gets married. Not only Sis Kyŏng-ja but almost all the other people in town treat him in a slightly scornful manner, as if to treat a child, because he's known to have gone a bit off his head. It's hard to say when and how it all started, but there's no doubt that he is different from other ordinary people. Mr. Mongdal lives on the third floor of the Rose of Sharon Row Houses. On the veranda of his place are unusually many flower

나 많지만 우리는 엄연히 친구다. 믿지 않겠지만 내게는 스물일곱짜리 남자친구가 또 하나 있다. 우리 집 옆, 형제 슈퍼의 김반장이 바로 또 하나의 내 친구인데 그는 원미동 23통 5반의 반장으로 누구보다도 씩씩하고 재미있는 사람이었다. 나는 매일같이 슈퍼 앞의 비치파라솔 의자에 앉아 그와 함께 낄낄거리는 재미로 하루를 보내다시피 하였는데 요즘은 내가 의자에 앉아 있어도 전처럼 웃기는 소리를 해 주거나 쭈쭈바 따위를 건네주는 법 없이 다소 퉁명스러워졌다. 그 까닭도 나는 환히 알고 있지만 모르는 척하는 수밖에. 우리 집 셋째 딸 선옥이 언니가 지난달에 서울 이모 집으로 훌쩍 떠나 버렸기 때문인 것이다. 김반장이 선옥이 언니랑 좋아지내는 것은 온 동네가 다 아는 일이지만 선옥이 언니 마음이 요새 좀 싱숭생숭하더니 기어이는 이모네가 하는 옷가게를 도와준다고 서울로 가 버렸다. 선옥이 언니는 얼굴이 아주 예뻤다. 남들 말대로 개천에서 용이 났다고 해도 과언이 아닐 만큼 지지리 궁상인 우리 집에 두고 보기로는 아까운 판인데, 그 지지리 궁상이 지겨워 만날 뚱하던 언니였다.

참말이지 밝히고 싶지 않지만 우리 아버지는 청소부다. 아침 새벽부터 저녁 늦게까지 남의 집 쓰레기통만 뒤지고

pots and as many as three bird cages hanging. His family is rich enough to keep the air-conditioner on all day long in summer, which is rare in my town. His father is a herbal doctor and runs a clinic downtown. At his advanced age, his father married a young woman not long ago and just started to enjoy his remaining years, when the poet, his youngest son, moved his residence from his married older brother's to his father's. Madam Kohŭng at Kangnam Realtor's says that the poet's moving in with his newly-wed father and stepmother is in itself a foolish thing to do. However, I have no idea why it's a foolish thing for a son to move in with his father.

I am probably the only friend Mr. Mongdal has. He's twenty-seven, so he's twenty years older than I am; nonetheless, we're friends fair and square. Believe it or not, I have another twenty-seven-year-old male friend: Mr. Kim, the owner of Brothers Supermarket next to my house, who is also the head of the neighborhood association in charge of the residents of the fifth-ban, twenty-third-tong, Wŏnmi-dong. He is very gallant and fun to be with. I used to spend a whole day giggling with Mr. Kim, sitting on one of the chairs under the beach parasol

다니는 직업이라 몸에서 나는 냄새도 말할 수 없을 만큼 지독했다. 아버지만이 아니라 밝히고 싶지 않은 것이 또 있다. 큰언니는 경기도 양평으로 시집가서 농사꾼 아내가 되었으니 상관없지만 둘째 언니 이야기는 말하기가 부끄럽다. 둘째 언니는 처음에는 버스 안내양, 그다음에는 소시지 공장의 여공원, 그다음에는 다방에서 일하더니 돈 버는 일에 극성인 성격대로 지금은 구로동 어디에서 스물여섯 살의 처녀가 대폿집을 열고 있다. 언젠가 한번 가 봤더니 키가 멀대같이 큰 남자가 하나뿐인 방에서 위통을 벗어 붙인 채 잠들어 있고 언니는 그 옆에서 엎드려 주간지를 뒤적이고 있지 않은가. 그만한 정도로도 나는 일이 되어 가는 모양을 알 수가 있었다.

우리 엄마와 청소부 아버지는 딸년들이야 시집보낼 만큼만 가르치면 족하다고 언니들을 모두 중학교까지만 보냈는데 웬일인지 선옥이 언니만 고등학교를 보냈었다. 그래서 더 골치이긴 하지만. 기껏 고등학교까지 나왔으니 공장은 싫다, 차라리 영화배우가 되는 편이 낫다고 우거지상을 피우던 언니가 김반장네의 콧구멍 같은 가게가 성에 찰 리 없을 것이었다. 이제 겨우 일곱 살짜리가, 사실은 그보다야 많지만 왜 나이 많은 떠꺼머리총각들하고만

in front of the supermarket. Recently, however, he's become rather curt to me. He no longer tells funny stories or offers a Chu-Chu ice-bar to me sitting under the parasol. I know the reason only too well, but I have no choice but to pretend ignorance. My third eldest sister Sŏn-ok suddenly left for our aunt's house in Seoul last month. The whole town knows that Mr. Kim and Sŏn-ok have been dating. Then of late, Sŏn-ok became a little distracted, and in the end left the town for Seoul, saying that she would like to help out at Aunt's clothes shop. Sŏn-ok has a very pretty face. Given the looks of my parents, I dare say, it's a case of a black hen laying white eggs. She is too pretty to remain stuck in our wretched household, which she has always been sick of and depressed about.

I really don't want to say this, but my father is a garbage man. He stinks like hell since he handles one garbage can after another from dawn till late in the evening. There is another family member I'd rather not talk about: my second eldest sister. Unlike my eldest sister who is married to a farmer in Yangpyŏng, Kyŏnggi-Province, my second eldest sister makes me feel ashamed of talking about her. At first, she worked as a bus conductor, then a

어울리는지 이상할 터이나 그것은 결코 내 책임이 아니었다. 단짝인 소라를 비롯하여 몇 명의 친구들이 작년과 올해에 걸쳐 모두 국민학교에 입학해 버렸고, 좀 어려도 아쉰 대로 놀아 볼 만한 아이들까지 깡그리 유치원에 다니기 때문에 아침밥 먹구 나오면 원미동 거리에는 이제 두어 살짜리 코흘리개들밖에 남지 않는 것이다. 설령 오후가 되어도 사정은 마찬가지였다. 끼리끼리만 통하는 아이들이 좀처럼 놀이에 끼워 주지 않기 때문에 나는 그만 홀로 뚝 떨어져 나와 외계인처럼 어성버성한 아이가 되어 버렸다. 우리 동네에는 값이 싼 유치원도 많고 피아노 교습소도 두 군데나 있지만 엄마는 꿈쩍도 하지 않는다. 단칸방에 살아도 모두들 유치원에 보내느라고 아침마다 법석인데 나는 이날 이때껏 유희 한번 제대로 배워 보지 못한 것이다. 아버지가 남의 집 쓰레기통에서 주워 온 그림책이나 고장 난 장난감이야 지천으로 널렸지만 이제는 그런 것들에는 흥미도 없으니 아무래도 나는 어른이 다 된 모양이었다.

몽달씨와 친구가 된 것은 올 봄, 바로 외계인 같던 시절이었다. 형제슈퍼 앞에서 어슬렁거리며 김반장이 언제나 말동무가 되어 주려나 눈치만 보고 있는데 바로 내 뒤에

laborer at a sausage factory, then a waitress in a coffee shop, and finally, at the age of twenty-six, she started to run a sort of grogshop somewhere in Kuro-dong, which is, in fact, in line with her money-grubbing personality. I visited her once and saw a tall man sleeping, naked from waist up, and my sister flipping through a weekly magazine lying on her stomach beside the sleeping man. Instantly, I was able to size up what had happened to my sister.

My parents think that junior high school education is good enough to marry off their daughters. So, the first two daughters graduated from junior high, and that was it. However, for some reason, my parents allowed Sŏn-ok to graduate from senior high. Since the graduation, she's been saying that she doesn't want to work in a factory, because she now has a high school diploma, and that she would rather become an actress. It's true that she's become a headache, but there's no way that my sister would settle for Mr. Kim and his tiny supermarket. Some may think it strange for a seven-year-old, or even eight or nine-year-old, to hang out with much older unmarried men, but it's not my fault. My best friend, So-ra, and several other friends all entered elemen-

똑같은 자세로 김반장 눈치를 보는 몽달씨가 있었다. 염색한 작업복 주머니에서 꼬깃꼬깃한 종이를 펼쳐 들고 주춤주춤 내 옆의 빈 의자에 앉은 그가 "경옥아" 하고 내 이름을 불렀을 때 정말이지 나는 기절할 정도로 놀랐다. 좀 바보이고 약간 돌았다고 생각했으므로 언젠가는 그가 보는 앞에서도 "헤이, 몽달귀신!" 하고 놀려댄 적도 있었던 나였다. 놀라서 입을 쩌억 벌리고 있는 내게 그가 다음에 건넨 말은 더욱 기가 찼다.

"너는 나더러 개새끼, 개새끼라고만 그러는구나……."

나는 눈을 둥그렇게 떴다. 몽달귀신이라고 부른 적은 있지만 결코, '참말이지 하늘에 맹세코' 그를 개새끼라고 부른 적은 없었다. 그래서 나는 나도 모르게 고개를 마구 저어댔다. 그런 나를 보는지 마는지 그는 계속해서 말했다. 너는 나더러 개새끼, 개새끼라고만 그러는구나…….

지금 생각해도 참 어이가 없는 노릇이지만, 세상에 그게 바로 시라는 것이었다. 김반장이 몽달씨에게 시를 쓴다 하니 멋있는 시를 한 수 지어 보라고 했다는 것이다. 그 청을 받고 몽달씨는 밤새 끙끙거리며 시를 쓰려 했으나 도무지 마음먹은 대로 되지 않아 어느 유명한 시인의 시를 베껴 왔는데 그 구절이 바로 그 시의 마지막이라고

tary schools last year and this year. Further, all those kids, who are younger than me but still fun to play with, go to kindergarten. Coming out of my house after breakfast, all I can find is snotty two or three-year-olds. It doesn't change much even in the after-noon. The elementary school kids flock together and won't let me join them in their play. I'm always left all alone, feeling as if I were an extraterrestrial. My town has many kindergartens with reasonable rates of tuition and two places where kids can take piano lessons, but my mother won't budge an inch. Even those who live in one-room homes bustle about every morning sending their kids to kinder-gartens. As for me, I've never learned so much as a children's dance sequence. Of course, my father brings home piles of picture books and broken toys he's found in other people's garbage cans. Nevertheless, I'm not at all interested in them; ten to one I've all grown out of them.

It was in the spring of this year when I, cut off from the world of children, got acquainted with Mr. Mongdal. I was hanging about in front of Brothers Supermarket, stealing glances at Mr. Kim in the hope that he would speak to me. Suddenly, I noticed Mr. Mongdal standing right behind me, also

했다.

"예끼, 이 사람아. 내가 언제 자네더러 개새끼, 개새끼 그랬는가?"

김반장은 으레 그럴 줄 알았다는 듯 몽달씨 어깨를 툭 치며 빈정대고 말았지만 나의 놀라움은 쉽게 가시지 않았다. 기억을 못해서 그렇지 그를 향해 개새끼, 라고 욕을 한 적이 꼭 있었던 것같이만 생각될 지경이었다. 김반장이야 뭐라건 말건 몽달씨는 그날 이후 며칠간은 개새끼 시를 외우고 다녔고 나는 김반장 외에 몽달씨까지도 내 친구로 해야겠다고 속으로 결심해 두었다. 시인하고 친구가 된다는 것은 구멍가게 주인과 친구가 되는 것보다는 훨씬 근사했으니까.

그렇긴 했으나 약간 돈 사내와 오랜 시간을 어울려 다닐 만큼 나는 간이 크지 못했다. 게다가 김반장은 마음이 내키면 언제라도 알사탕이나 쭈쭈바를 내놓을 수 있지만 몽달씨는 그런 면으로는 영 젬병이었다. 그는 오로지 시에 대하여 말하고 시를 생각하고 시를 함께 외우자는 요구밖에는 몰랐다. 그에게는 시가 전부였다. 바람이 불면 '풀잎에 바람 스치는 소리' 때문에 가슴이 아프고, 수녀가 지나가면 문득 "열일곱 개의, 또는 스물한 개의 단추들이

trying to attract Mr. Kim's attention. He took out a crumpled piece of paper from the pocket of his dyed fatigue pants and unfolded it. Then he hesitantly sat down on a chair next to mine and out of the blue, called me by my name. Hearing him call me "Kyŏng-ok," I was so flabbergasted that I nearly fainted. Then I remembered yelling at him once, "Hey, Mongdal Ghost," thinking that he was kind of simple and crazy. So, suddenly spoken to by him like that, I couldn't help staring at him with my mouth agape. The next thing he said to me was much more shocking.

"You keep calling me 'son of a bitch,' 'son of a bitch.'"

My eyes widened. Yes, I'd called him "Mongdal Ghost," but never, I swear, had I called him "son of a bitch." So, I vigorously shook my head involuntarily. He didn't seem to notice my denial at all and kept repeating the same thing, "You keep calling me 'son of a bitch,' 'son of a bitch.'"

To my greatest surprise, that was what's called a poem. I still get knocked cold whenever I recall that episode. According to Mr. Mongdal, Mr. Kim had told him the previous day since he was writing poems, perhaps he could write a fine one for Mr.

그녀를 가두었다"라고 부르짖었다. 그는 하루 종일이라도 유명한 시인들의 시를 외울 수 있었다. 그것만이 아니었다. 외운 시구절만 가지고 몇 시간이라도 대화를 할 수 있다고 그가 말하였다. 그게 바로 시적 대화라고 가르쳐 주기도 하였다. 그러기 위해서 그는 밤새도록 시를 읽는다고 하였다. 몽달씨는 밤이 되면 엎드려 시를 외우고, 다음날이면 그 시로써 말하는 사람이었다.

시를 빼고 나면 나와 마찬가지로 몽달씨도 심심한 사람이었다. 낮 동안에는 꼼짝없이 젊은 새어머니와 한집에서 지내야 하기 때문에 끊임없이 동네를 빙빙 돌면서 시간을 떼워 나갔다. 내가 김반장과 마주 앉아 별로 새로울 것도 없는 이야기를 하다 보면 어느샌가 슬쩍 다가와 약간 구부정한 허리로 의자에 주저앉곤 하는 몽달씨는 나보다 훨씬 강렬하게 김반장의 친구가 되었으면 하는 소망을 품고 있는 것처럼 보였다. 우리들은 제법 뜨거운 한낮 동안 각기 편한 자세로 앉아 신문을 읽거나 졸거나 하는 무료한 시간을 보내다가 막걸리 손님이라도 들이닥치면 몽달씨와 나는 재빨리 의자를 비워 주곤 김반장이 바삐 설치는 모양을 우두커니 바라보곤 하였다. 김반장은 몽달씨가 시가 어쩌구 하며 이야기를 꺼내기라도 할라치면 대번에

Kim himself. At the request, Mr. Mongdal stayed up all night trying to write a poem, to no avail. So, he decided to copy a famous poet's work and brought it to Mr. Kim; and, the phrase with which he shocked me to death was the last part of the poem.

"C'mon, Man! When did I ever call you 'son of a bitch'?"

After hearing the poem, Mr. Kim patted him on the shoulder, as if to say, "What on earth did I expect from you?" Unlike Mr. Kim, the shock was not to leave me any time soon. I almost felt that I had actually called him 'son of a bitch' and forgotten all about it. Regardless of what Mr. Kim thought of the poem, Mr. Mongdal wandered about reciting the son-of-a-bitch poem and I determined to make Mr. Mongdal, as well as Mr. Kim, my friend. It seemed more glamorous to make friends with a poet than with a small shop owner.

Having said that, I must confess I wasn't brave enough to hang out with a slightly crazy man for a long time. Moreover, Mr. Kim could give me some candies or a Chu-Chu ice-bar, if he wanted to, while Mr. Mongdal had absolutely nothing to offer me. He only talked about poetry, thought about poetry, and asked me to memorize poems together with him.

딴소리를 해서 입막음을 하기 때문에 몽달씨도 김반장 앞에서는 도통 시에 대한 말을 입에 올리지 않았다. 대신에 내가 원미동 시인의 '시적 대화'를 끊임없이 듣는 형편이었다.

그때까지만 해도 몽달씨보다는 김반장과 함께 있는 것이 더 좋았었다. 김반장이 그 커다란 손바닥으로 내 엉덩이를 철썩 치면서 "어이, 경옥이 처제!" 하고 불러 주면 기분이 그럴싸해서 저절로 웃음이 비어져 나왔고 가끔가다 오토바이 뒷좌석에 앉아 함께 배달을 나가기라도 할라치면 피아노 배우러 가던 계집애들이 손가락을 입에 물고 부러워 죽겠다는 듯이 나를 바라봐 줬었다. 김반장이 말 많은 원미동 여자들 누구하고도 사이좋게 지내면서 야채에다 생선까지 떼어다 수월찮게 재미를 보는 것을 잘 아는 고흥댁 아주머니도 "선옥이가 인물만 좀 훤할 뿐이지 그 집안 꼬라지로 봐서 김반장이면 횡재한 거야" 하면서 은근히 선옥이 언니를 비아냥거렸다. 흥, 나는 고흥댁 아주머니의 마음도 알아맞힐 수 있다. 선옥이 언니보다 한 살 많은 딸이 하나 있는데 인물이 좀 제멋대로인 것이 아줌마의 속을 뒤집어 놓은 것이다. 그러면서도 지난번엔 김반장 같은 사위나 얼른 봐야 될 것 아니냐는 은혜 할머

Poetry was everything to him. When the wind blew, his heart ached because of the "sound of the wind grazing through the grass." When a nun passed by, he yelled out of nowhere, "Seventeen or twenty-one buttons have caged her." He was able to recite famous poems all day long, if he wanted to. That was not all. He said he could make hours of conversation using all the poems he had learned by heart, which was called a "poetic dialog." In order to be able to do so, he stayed up night after night, reading poems. By night, Mr. Mongdal memorized poems, lying on his stomach, and by day, he practiced the poetic dialog.

Without poetry, Mr. Mongdal was as much a bored person as I was. During the day, he had no choice but to stay with his young stepmother in the same house. So, he wandered all over our town to kill time. Whenever Mr. Kim and I were chatting about some trifles, Mr. Mongdal would appear and sit down on a chair next to ours, his back hunched up. He seemed to have a stronger desire than mine to be Mr. Kim's friend. We would sit through the considerable heat of the mid-day, reading or dozing off in our respective comfortable postures. When customers came to drink rice wine, Mr. Mongdal and I

니 말에는 가당찮게도 코웃음 쳤었다.

"요새 시상에 뭐 부모가 무슨 상관 있답뎌? 그래도 갸가 보는 눈이 높아서 엥간한 남자는 말도 못 꺼내게 하요잉. 저기 은행 대리가 중매를 넣어 왔는디도 돌아보도 않습니다. 전문학교일망정 대학물도 일 년 남짓 보았고 해서, 아는 게 아주 많다요."

그런 말을 들을 때마다 나는 목구멍이 근질거려서 견딜 수가 없었다. 왜 목구멍이 근질거리는가 하면 나는 또 다른 비밀을 하나 알고 있기 때문이었다. 이것은 정말 특급 비밀인데 만약에 이 사실을 고흥댁 아주머니가 알았다가는 어떻게 수습이 될는지 내가 더 걱정인 판이다.

복덕방집 딸 동아 언니가 누구와 좋아지내는가는 아마 나밖에 모르는 일일 것이다. 지난봄에 소라네 집에 놀러 갔다가 우연히 알게 된 사실로 소라조차도 영 모르고 있으니 나 혼자만 끙끙 앓다 말아야 할 것이긴 하지만, 그날 이후 복덕방 식구들만 만나면 내가 더 안절부절못했다. 여태까지 누구에게도 털어놓지 않은 말이라 좀 망설여지긴 하지만 아이, 할 수 없다, 이야기를 꺼냈으니 털어놓을 밖에. 동아 언니는 소라네 대신설비에서 소라 아빠의 일을 거들어 주는 노가다 청년하고 연애를 하는 판이다. 그

quickly surrendered our chairs to them and vacantly watched Mr. Kim busy working. Whenever Mr. Mongdal brought up the subject of poetry, Mr. Kim would immediately shut him up with another subject. So, Mr. Mongdal stopped talking about poetry with Mr. Kim altogether. Instead, I found myself listening to Wŏnmi-dong poet's endless poetic dialog.

Up until then, I liked talking to Mr. Kim more than listening to Mr. Mongdal. Whenever Mr. Kim playfully smacked me on the bottom with the big hand of his and said, "Hey, Kyŏng-ok, my sister-in-law," it rang so true that a smile appeared around my mouth despite myself. Once in a while, he would let me sit in the back seat of his motorbike on his delivery trip, which had the girls on their way to piano lessons stop and watch me, drooling. Mr. Kim was getting along well with the talkative Wŏnmi-dong women and making considerable profits by supplying them fresh vegetables and fish directly from wholesalers. Madam Kohŭng knew about it and made a sarcastic remark about my sister Sŏn-ok, "All Sŏn-ok has is her good looks. Considering the fix her family's in, Mr. Kim should be considered a windfall." Humph! I knew what was on her mind. She had a daughter a year older than Sŏn-ok,

것도 보통 사이가 아니다. 지난 봄날, 소라네 집에 갔다가 소라가 보이지 않아 무심코 모퉁이를 돌아 나와 옆구리 창으로 가게를 기웃 들여다보니 그 두 남녀가 딱 붙어 앉아서 이상한 짓을 하고 있지 않은가. 동아 언니는 그렇다 치고 청년은 땀까지 뻘뻘 흘리면서 언니의 머리통을 꽉 껴안고 있었는데 좀 무섭기도 하였다.

이야기가 괜히 옆으로 흘렀지만 아무튼 선옥이 언니가 김반장 같은 신랑감을 차 버린 것은 좀 아쉬운 일이기도 하였다. 김반장이야 아직도 미련을 버리지 못하고 있는 터라 나만 보면 지금도 언니가 왔는가를 묻기에 여념이 없었다. 허나 선옥이 언니는 처음 떠날 때도 그랬지만 요사이 한 번씩 집에 들를 적에도 형제슈퍼 쪽은 쳐다보지도 않는다. 어떨 때는 "어휴, 저 거지발싸개 같은 자식"이라고 욕도 막 내뱉는데 어떻게 알았는지 이모네 옷가게로 심심하면 전화질이라고 이를 갈았다. 가만히 눈치를 보아하니 선옥이 언니도 요새 새 남자가 생긴 것 같고 전과 달리 아무 데서나 속옷을 훌렁훌렁 벗어던지며 옷을 갈아입는데, 그 속옷이 요사무사하게 생겨서 내 눈을 달뜨게 하곤 했다. 좀 만져라도 볼라치면 언니는 내 손을 탁 때려버렸다.

whose looks were far from approvable and upset her mother's peace of mind. That being the case, though, when Ŭn-hye's grandmother told her that she should hurry and get a son-in-law like Mr. Kim, she ridiculously sneered at the advice,

"These days, who listens to her parents? Anyway, my daughter aims so high that she won't even hear of ordinary men. The assistant manager at the bank over there sent a matchmaker, but she wouldn't even think about it. She attended a college for over a year, you see. Though it was a vocational college, she learned so much there."

Whenever I heard her make that kind of remarks, I had such a hard time holding down the tickles in my throat. The unbearable tickles stemmed from the secret that I had been keeping. The sheer magnitude of the top secret was such that I worried seriously about the consequences once Madam Kohŭng got wind of it.

No one else knew whom the daughter of the realtor, Tong-a, was in love with. Last spring, I went to So-ra's to play with her and happened upon the couple. Even So-ra herself didn't have a clue about it, so I figured that I had to keep it all bottled up inside me. Nevertheless, I couldn't help feeling anx-

"어때, 이쁘지? 경옥이 넌 이런 것 처음 보지? 이거, 모두 선물 받은 거다."

끈으로 아슬아슬하게 꿰매 놓은 저런 팬티 따위를 선물하는 치도 우습지만 그것을 자랑하는 언니는 더욱 밉상이어서 그럴 때면 속도 모르는 김반장이 불쌍해지기도 하였다.

몽달씨가 있음으로 인하여 김반장의 주가가 더 올라가는 점도 있었다. 나야 어린애니까 형제슈퍼의 비치파라솔 아래서 어슬렁거려도 흉볼 사람은 없지만 동갑내기인 몽달씨가 하는 일도 없이 가게 근처를 빙빙 돌면서 어떨 때는 나와 같이 쭈쭈바나 쪽쪽 빨고 있으면 오가는 동네 어른들마다 혀를 끌끌 찼다.

"대학 다닐 때까진 저러지 않았대요. 저도 잘은 모르지만 학교에서 잘렸대나 봐요. 뭐 뻔하죠. 요새 대학생들 짓거린. 그리곤 곧장 군대에 갔는데 제대하고부턴 사람이 저리 됐어요. 언제나 중얼중얼 시를 외운다는데 확 미쳐버린 것도 아니구, 아주 죽겠어요."

몽달씨 새어머니 되는 이가 김반장에게 하소연하는 소리였다. 형제슈퍼 단골인 그녀는 '아주 죽겠어요'가 입버릇이었다.

ious every time I ran across the realtor's family. Even now, I hesitate to reveal the secret that I've never shared with anybody. Yet, since I've already brought up the subject, I might as well take it all out of my chest. Tong-a has been in a relationship with a part-time laborer helping out at So-ra's father's shop, Taeshin Hardware. Their relationship involves much more than the usual going-to-the-movies-together kind of dating. On that particular spring day, So-ra wasn't home, so I casually rounded the corner and looked in the side window to find the realtor's daughter and her lover sitting glued to each other, doing strange things. It was hard to see Tong-a's face, but the young man was sweating profusely, holding Tong-a's head tightly in his arms. The scene scared me a little.

I've digressed from the story of Mr. Mongdal. Anyway, it was a shame that Sŏn-ok turned down a suitor like Mr. Kim. Unable to give up my sister, Mr. Kim obsessively continued to ask me if my sister was back home. However, Sŏn-ok, just as she had done when she first left for Seoul, never even cast a glance in the direction of the supermarket when she came home for a visit every now and then. Sometimes, she even called him colorful names. I

"내 체면을 봐서라도 옷이나 좀 깨끗이 입고 나다니면 좋으련만, 아주 죽겠어요."

말이 났으니 말이지 그 옷차림은 형제슈퍼의 심부름꾼 복장으로 딱 걸맞았다. 종일 의자에서 빈둥거리기라도 지겨운지라 우리는 곧잘 가게 일도 마다 않고 거들었었다. 우리 둘이서 기껏 머리를 짜내어 하는 일이란 게 고무호스로 가게 앞에 물을 뿌려 주는 정도였다. 포장이 덜 된 가게 앞길의 먼지 제거를 위해서나 여름 땡볕을 좀 무디게 하는 방법으로는 그 이상도 없어서 김반장도 우리의 일을 기꺼이 바라봐 주고 일이 끝나면 기분이란 듯 요구르트 한 개씩을 던져 주기도 하였다.

그러다 차츰차츰 몽달씨 몫의 일이 하나둘 늘어 갔는데 가게 앞 청소나 빈 박스를 지하실 창고에 쟁이는 일 혹은 막걸리 손님 심부름 따위가 그것으로, 몽달씨가 거드는 일이 많으면 많을수록 김반장은 더욱 의젓해지고 몽달씨는 자꾸 초라하게 비추어지는 게 나에겐 참으로 이상한 일이었다. 김반장도 그걸 모르지는 않았을 것이다. 그래서 언젠가는 아주 정색을 하고서 몽달씨 어깨를 꽉 껴안더니 이렇게 말하기도 하였다.

"자네 같은 시인에게 이런 일만 시키려니 미안하이. 자

heard her grind out, "Ugh, that filthy scum!" while she was complaining about Mr. Kim who managed somehow to get hold of the phone number of Aunt's clothes shop and called her whenever he wanted to. I sensed that Sŏn-ok had gotten herself a new boyfriend. She changed under clothes everywhere, dropping them here and there, which was out of character for her. Further, those under clothes were so flashy that they dazzled my eyes. When I tried to touch them, my sister slapped me on the back of my hand.

"What d'you think? Aren't they pretty? I bet you've never seen anything like these before. They were given to me as presents."

It was repulsive of the guy to give her that kind of panties, held together precariously only with thin spaghetti cords, as a present. My sister, however, who showed them off, was more disgusting. I couldn't help sympathizing with Mr. Kim who knew nothing about what was on my sister's mind.

Anyway, Mr. Mongdal helped improve Mr. Kim's reputation, if indirectly. I was a child, so no one would speak ill of me hanging out under the beach parasol in front of Brothers Supermarket. As to Mr. Mongdal, however, it was a different story. The

네는 확실히 시인은 시인이야. 언제 바쁘지 않을 때는 정말이지 자네 시를 찬찬히 읽어 봄세. 이래봬도 학교 다닐 때 위문편지는 내가 도맡아 써 주곤 했던 실력이니까."

그러면 몽달씨는 더욱 신이 나서 생선 잘라 주는 통나무 도마까지 깔끔히 씻어 내고 널브러져 있는 채소들을 다듬고 하면서 분주히 설치는 것이었다. 하지만 이제껏 몽달씨의 시 노트를 읽어 본 적이 없는 김반장이었다. 몽달씨가 짐짓 아직 자기 시는 읽을 만하지 못하니 유명한 시인들의 시나 읽어 보지 않겠느냐고 구깃구깃 접은 종이를 꺼낼라치면 김반장은 온갖 핑계를 다 대서라도 줄행랑을 치면서 그가 보지 않은 틈을 타 머리 위에 대고 손가락으로 빙글, 동그라미를 그려 보였다. 그것도 모르고 몽달씨는 언제라도 김반장에게 들려줄 수 있는 꼬깃꼬깃한 종이쪽지들을 호주머니마다 가득 넣어 가지고 다녔다. 그때쯤엔 나도 몽달씨의 시적 대화에는 질려 있어서 덩달아 자리를 피했고 김반장을 따라 머리 위에 손가락으로 동그라미를 그려댔다. 약간, 아니 혹시는 아주 많은 돈 원미동 시인은 그래도 여전히 형제슈퍼의 심부름꾼 꼬마처럼 다소곳이 잔심부름을 도맡아가지고 있었다.

분명히 말하지만 보름 전쯤 그 사건이 일어날 때까지만

elders of the town would click their tongues when they passed by and saw Mr. Mongdal, the same age as Mr. Kim, loitering around the supermarket doing nothing or sometimes sucking on a Chu-Chu ice-bar alongside me.

"I heard that he wasn't like that while in college. I'm not quite sure, but he might have been expelled from the college. It seems pretty obvious why. You know, what college students get involved in these days. After that, he was immediately enlisted for military service. It was right after his discharge when he suddenly changed. He says he's trying to memorize poems, muttering them on and on. It's not like he's gone completely mad, either. That is why it's all the more unnerving!" complained Mr. Mongdal's step-mother, one of Brothers Supermarket's old customers, to Mr. Kim. "It's just so unnerving" was her stock phrase,

"I wish he would dress more neatly and help me save my face. It's just so unnerving!"

Come to think of it, his clothes were perfect to be an errand boy at the supermarket. In fact, bored with loafing about, we didn't mind at all helping out with the chores at the supermarket. Our enthusiasm notwithstanding, all we could think of was hosing

해도 나는 김반장이 내 셋째 형부가 되어 주길 은근히 바라고 있었다. 농사짓는 큰형부는 워낙이 나이가 많아 늙은 아버지 같아서 싫었고 둘째 언니야 아직 공식적으로 처녀니까 별 볼일 없는 데다 형부다운 형부는 선옥이 언니가 결혼해야 생길 터이니 기왕이면 김반장 같은 남자가 형부가 되길 바란 것이었다. 하기야 넷째 언니도 시방 같은 공장에 다니는 사내와 눈이 맞아서 부쩍 세수하는 시간이 길어지긴 했지만 그래 봤자 앞차가 두 대나 밀려 있으니 어림도 없었다. 선옥이 언니와 김반장이 결혼하면 누가 뭐래도 나는 형제슈퍼에 진득이 붙어 있을 수 있는 자격을 갖게 되는 셈이었다. 기분이 내키면 삼백 원짜리 빵빠레를 먹은들 어떠하랴. 오밀조밀 늘어놓은 온갖 과자와 초콜릿과 사탕이 모두 내 손아귀에 있다, 라고 생각하면 어쩔 수 없이 나는 흐물흐물 기분이 좋아졌다.

그런데 정확히 열나흘 전의 그 일로 인하여 나는 김반장과 형제슈퍼의 잡다한 군것질감을 한꺼번에 포기하였다. 모르긴 몰라도 이런 나의 처사는 백번 옳을 것이었다. 그 사건의 처음과 끝을 빠짐없이 지켜본 유일한 목격자는 나 하나뿐이었지만 그렇다고 내가 본 것을 누군가에게도 늘어놓지는 않았다. 웬일인지 그 일에 관해서는 입도 뻥

the unpaved ground in front of the store. Fortunately, it happened to be the most effective way to settle the dust and take the edge off the mid-summer heat. So, Mr. Kim watched us work approvingly, and when the job was done, he would toss couple of yogurt bottles to us.

Gradually, Mr. Mongdal's share of work increased to include cleaning the front yard of the store, stacking empty boxes in the basement storage, running errands for drinking customers, etc. I couldn't understand why the more Mr. Mongdal worked there, the more dignified Mr. Kim became and the shabbier Mr. Mongdal looked. I think Mr. Kim wasn't ignorant of it either; one day, Mr. Kim with a serious face put his arms tightly around Mr. Mongdal's shoulders and said,

"I'm sorry to ask a poet like you to do the kinds of work you do here. You're certainly a poet. When I'm not busy, I'll carefully read your poems one by one. I may not look it, but I used to write reams of consolatory letters to soldiers on behalf of my schoolmates."

Then, Mr. Mongdal became so much encouraged that he busied himself harder, cleaning the chopping board used to cut fish and the vegetables left

긋하기 싫었다. 그런 채로 나 혼자서만 김반장을 형부감에서 제외시켜 버렸던 것이다. 또 하나, 아주 용기를 필요로 하는 일이었지만 그날 이후로는 김반장이 내 엉덩이를 철썩 두들기며 어이, 우리 경옥이 처제 어쩌구 할 때는 단호하게 그를 뿌리치고 도망 나와 버리곤 하였다. 물론 그가 내미는 쭈쭈바도 받아먹지 않았다.

그 사건은 초여름 밤 열 시가 넘어서 일어났다. 그날은 낮부터 티격태격해대던 엄마와 아버지와의 말싸움이 저녁에 이르러서는 본격적으로 시작되었었다. 넷째 언니는 야간 조업이 있다고 늘상 열두 시가 다 되어야 돌아오는 처지라 만만한 나만 엄마의 분풀이 대상이 되어서 낮부터 적잖이 욕설도 들어 먹었던 차였다. 싸우는 이유도 뭐 그리 대단한 게 아니었다. 아버지가 쓰레기 속에서 주워 온 십팔금 목걸이를 맥주 네 병으로 맞바꾸어 간단히 목을 축이고 돌아왔노라는 말을 내뱉은 뒤부터 엄마의 잔소리가 시작된 게 원인이었다. 새삼 길게 이야기할 것도 없고 요지는 맥주 네 병으로 홀랑 마셔 버리느니 지 여편네 목에 걸어 주면 무슨 동티가 날까 봐 그랬느냐는 아우성이었다. 엄마가 지금 손가락에 끼고 있는, 약간 색이 변한 십팔금 반지도 아버지가 주워 온 것인데 짜장 목걸이까지

untouched by Mr. Kim. However, I knew that Mr. Kim had never opened Mr. Mongdal's poetry notebook. Whenever Mr. Mongdal tried to take out a crumpled piece of paper, offering to show Mr. Kim some of the poems written by famous poets—since his poems were not yet good enough, Mr. Kim would make all kinds of excuses to escape and looked at me making circles over his head with his forefinger behind Mr. Mongdal's back. Oblivious to it all, Mr. Mongdal always carried many folded papers in all of his pockets so that he could read them to Mr. Kim any time he was ready to listen. By then, I got sick of the poetic dialog with Mr. Mongdal, so I, too, avoided him and made circles over my head with my forefinger, mimicking Mr. Kim. The slightly, or seriously, insane Wŏnmi-dong poet continued to do all the chores at Brothers Supermarket, as if he were Mr. Kim's obedient errand boy.

I want to make it clear that I had, deep down, hoped to have Mr. Kim as my third brother-in-law until the incident occurred about half a month ago. My first brother-in-law, a farmer, is so old that he looks like my old father. My second eldest sister is still single, at least on paper. So, it seemed that I

세트로 갖출 뻔한 기회를 놓쳐서 엄마는 단단히 약이 올랐다. 그러던 말싸움이 저녁에 가서는 기어이 험악한 욕설과 아버지의 손찌검으로 이어지길래 나는 언제나처럼 슬그머니 집을 빠져나와 비어 있는 형제슈퍼의 노천 의자에 앉아 있었다. 가끔씩 있는 일로서 머지않아 아버지가 엄마를 케이오로 때려눕힌 뒤 코를 골며 잠들어 버릴 것이었다. 그다음엔 눈물 콧물 다 짜낸 엄마가 발을 질질 끌며 거리로 나와 경옥아!를 목청껏 부를 판이었다. 그때나 되어 못 이기는 척 들어가 잠자리에 누워 버리면 내일 아침의 새날이 올 것이 분명하였다.

집에서 나온 것이 아홉 시쯤, 그래서 김반장도 가겟방에 놓은 흑백텔레비전으로 저녁 뉴스를 시청하느라고 내가 나온 것도 모르고 있었다. 장가들면 색시가 컬러텔레비전을 해 올 것이므로 굳이 바꿀 필요 없다고 고물 텔레비전으로 견디어 내는 김반장의 등허리를 흘낏 쳐다보고 나는 신발까지 벗고 의자 위에 냉큼 올라앉았다. 잠이 오면 탁자에 엎드려 한숨 졸고 있어 볼 생각으로 나는 가물가물 감기는 눈을 비비며 이리저리 몸을 뒤척이고 있었다. 거리는 그날따라 유난히 한산했고 지물포나 사진관도 일찌감치 아크릴 간판에 불을 꺼 둔 채였다. 우리정육점

would get a brother-in-law true to the name only when Sŏn-ok got married. I preferred to have a man like Mr. Kim as my brother-in-law if possible. As a matter of fact, my youngest sister has just fallen in love with a guy who's working in the same factory as she. That's why she's taking her time washing her face these days. In my opinion, however, she shouldn't be overly ambitious, considering the two older cars to pull out before it becomes her turn. If Mr. Kim and Sŏn-ok got married, I would be entitled to hang out in the supermarket all the time. I could even eat one of those 300-wŏn Fanfare ice-bar whenever I felt like it. All kinds of cookies, chocolates, and candies neatly arranged on the shelves would be in my hands. Just thinking about it filled me with a sense of happiness.

However, the incident that took place exactly a fortnight ago forced me to give up all those goodies at Brothers Supermarket along with Mr. Kim. To the best of my knowledge, giving them up was the right thing to do. Although I was the only witness to the incident and I watched it from the beginning to the end, I didn't share it with anybody. For some reason, I didn't even want to open my mouth to talk about it. I simply eliminated Mr. Kim as a potential

은 휴일인지 셔터까지 내려져 있었다. 그 옆의 서울미용실은 경자 언니가 출퇴근을 하기 때문에 아홉 시만 되면 어김없이 불이 꺼진 채였다. 형제슈퍼에서 공단 쪽으로 난 길은 공터가 드문드문 박혀 있어서 원래 칠흑같이 어두웠다. 한 블록쯤 가야 세탁소가 내비치는 불빛이 쬐끔 새어 나올 뿐이고 포장도 안 된 울퉁불퉁한 소방 도로 옆으로는 자갈이며 벽돌 따위가 쌓여 있었다.

바로 그때 공단 쪽으로 가는 어두운 길에서 뭔가 비명 소리도 같고 욕지기를 참는 안간힘 같기도 한 소리가 들려왔다. 아니, 그때 나는 비몽사몽 졸음 속에서 헤매고 있었기 때문에 정확하게 어떤 소리를 들은 것은 아니었다. 이제 생각하면 그 순간에는 분명 잠에 흠뻑 취해 있었음이 분명했다. 그럼에도 불구하고 그 소리를 들었던 것처럼 생각된 것은 꿈속에까지 좇아와 악다구니를 벌이고 있는 엄마와 아버지의 모습을 보고 있었던 탓인지도 몰랐다. 하여간 허공을 가르는 비명 소리가 꿈속이었거나 생시였거나 간에 들려왔던 것은 사실이었다. 움찔 놀라며 눈을 떴을 때는 이미 누군가가 어둠을 뚫고 뛰쳐나와 필사적으로 가게를 향해 덮쳐 오는 중이었다. 그리고 그 뒤엔 덫에서 뛰쳐나온 노루 새끼를 붙잡으러 온 것이 확실

candidate for my brother-in-law. Further, I made another decision which took a great deal of my courage: whenever he smacked me on the bottom and said, "Hey, Kyŏng-ok, my sister-in-law, blah-blah," I decisively pushed him off and ran out of the supermarket. Needless to say, I stopped taking any of the Chu-Chu ice-bars he offered me.

The incident broke out after ten on an early summer night. Around noon, a squabble arose between my mother and father; and by the evening, it became quite serious. My youngest sister wouldn't come home until after midnight because of the overtime work at the factory. I became an easy target on whom my mother vented her anger all afternoon, using plenty of abusive language. The reason for their wrangle was really trivial. My father drank four bottles of beer in exchange for an 18-K gold necklace he had found in the garbage that day. When my mother heard of it, she started nagging. There's no need to go into details about her nagging; the gist is: Would it incur the divine wrath if he put it around his wife's neck, instead of guzzling it away with four bottles of beer? The slightly discolored 18-K gold ring on my mother's finger had also been scavenged by my father from the garbage. My

한 젊은 사내 둘이 가쁜 숨을 몰아쉬고 쫓아오고 있었다.

공교롭게도 나는 불빛에서 약간 비켜난 쪽의 의자에 앉아 있었기 때문에 그들의 눈에 띄지 않았다. 더욱 공교로웠던 것은 마침 가게 주변엔 아무도 없었다는 사실이었다. 때에 따라서는 비치파라솔 밑의 이 의자로는 턱이 없이 모자랄 만큼의 사람들이 왁자하게 모여 막걸리 타령을 벌이는 경우가 종종 있었다. 대게는 일을 끝내고 돌아가는 공사장의 인부들이었다. 그 사람들이 아니더라도 동네 사람 몇몇이 자주 이 의자에 앉아 밤바람을 쐬기도 했는데 그날은 아무도 없었다. 갑작스런 사태에 놀라 어리둥절하는 사이 도망자는 곧장 가게 안으로 들어가 버렸고 뒤쫓아 온 사람 중의 하나는 가게 앞에, 또 하나는 마악 가게 속으로 들어가는 중이어서 나는 그들의 모습을 비교적 자세히 볼 수 있었다.

"야, 이 새꺄! 이리 못 나와!"

가게 안으로 쫓아 들어가면서 소리치고 있는 사내는 빨간색의 소매 없는 러닝셔츠를 입고 있어서 땀에 번들거리는 어깻죽지가 엄청 우람하게 보였다.

"깽판 치기 전에 빨리 나오란 말야!"

가게 앞에 서서, 씩씩 가쁜 숨을 몰아쉬며 이마의 땀을

mother was completely exasperated at losing the chance to have a matching set of a ring and a necklace. Throughout the evening, the quarrel escalated into an exchange of horrible curses and finally into my father's beating my mother. As usual, I sneaked out of my house and went to Brothers Supermarket and sat on one of the chairs outside. My parents' wrangle was nothing new, so I knew that my father would K.O. my mother and fall asleep, snoring. Next, my mother, after crying her eyes out, would shuffle outside and call my name at the top of her lungs. Then I would, pretending reluctance, go back home and lie down in bed and wake up the next morning to face a new day.

It was around nine when I left home. Mr. Kim was in the room inside the supermarket. Engrossed in the evening news on his black and white TV, he didn't even notice me sitting outside. I threw a glance at Mr. Kim's back, recalling what he had once said: he didn't need to get a color TV set since his future bride would bring it. I took off my shoes and brought my feet up on the seat of the chair. I kept rubbing my sleepy eyes and tried to get into a comfortable position in case I fell asleep with my face on the table. The street was particularly desert-

훔치고 있는 사내는 두 개의 윗저고리를 한 손에 거머쥐고 있었다. 그도 당연히 러닝셔츠 바람이었지만 소매도 달린, 점잖은 흰색이었으므로 빨간 셔츠에 비해 훨씬 온순하게 보여졌다.

도대체 무슨 일일까. 호기심을 이기지 못한 나는 가게 옆구리의 샛문을 통해 안을 들여다보았다. 그새 사내의 발길에 차여 버린 도망자가 바닥에 엎어져 있었고 김반장이 만약을 위해 사내 주변의 맥주 박스를 방 안으로 져 나르면서 뭐라고 소리치고 있었다.

"김형, 김형…… 도와주세요."

쓰러진 남자의 입에서 이런 말이 가느다랗게 흘러나온 것은 그 순간이었다. 그와 동시에 빨간 셔츠의 사내가 다시 쓰러진 자의 등허리를 발로 꽉 찍어 눌렀다.

"이 새끼, 아는 사이요? 그러면 당신도 한번 맛 좀 볼 텐가?"

맥주병을 거꾸로 쳐들고 빨간 셔츠가 소리 질렀다. 김반장의 얼굴이 대번에 하얗게 질려 버렸다.

"무, 무슨 소리요? 난 몰라요! 상관없는 일에 말려들고 싶지 않으니까 나가서들 하시오."

그때 바닥에 쓰러져 버둥거리던 남자가 간신히 몸을 비

ed that night; and the acrylic signboards at both the paper shop and the photo studio were switched off early on. At Uri Butcher's, even the shutter was down. The lights in Seoul Beauty Salon were turned off exactly at nine, as usual, when Sis Kyŏng-ja went back home after work. The street leading to the industrial complex from Brothers Supermarket was as pitch-dark as ever with vacant lots interspersed along the way. I couldn't see the faint light of the dry-cleaner's, the only light on that stretch of street, from where I was. On either side of the unpaved, bumpy fire access were piles of gravel and bricks.

Suddenly, I heard a scream or someone holding back an urge to throw up. It was coming from the dark path leading to the industrial complex. To be precise, I shouldn't say I heard the sound because I was sound asleep at the moment. Nevertheless, I thought I heard it, perhaps because I was still watching the horrible fight between my mother and father who had stalked me even into my dream. Whether in a dream or in reality, the truth is that I heard the scream. When I was jerked out of my sleep and opened my eyes, I saw someone escaping the dark and running toward the supermarket at

틀고 일어섰다. 코피로 범벅이 된 얼굴이 슬쩍 드러나 보였는데 세상에, 그는 몽달씨임이 분명하였다. 그러고 보니 빛바랜 바지와 물들은 군용 점퍼 밑에 노상 껴입고 다니던 우중충한 남방셔츠가 틀림없는 몽달씨였다. 아까는 워낙 눈 깜짝할 사이에 가게 안으로 뛰어들었기 때문에 얼굴을 볼 겨를이 없었다.

"이 짜식, 왜 남의 집으로 토끼는 거야! 너 같은 놈은 좀 맞아야 돼."

흰 이를 드러내며 빨간 셔츠가 으르렁거렸다. 순간 몽달씨가 텔레비전이 왕왕거리고 있는 가겟방을 향해 튀었다. 방은 따로이 바깥쪽으로 난 출입구가 있었기 때문이었다. 그러나 몽달씨보다 더 빠른 동작으로 방문을 가로막아 버린 사람이 있었다. 바로 김반장이었다.

"나가요! 어서들 나가요! 싸우든가 말든가 장사 망치지 말고 어서 나가요!"

빨간 셔츠가 몽달씨의 목덜미를 확 낚아챘다. 개처럼 질질 끌려 나오는 몽달씨를 보더니 밖에 있던 흰 러닝셔츠가 찌익, 이빨 새로 침을 뱉어 냈다. 두 사람 다 술기운이 벌겋게 오른, 번들거리는 눈자위가 징그러웠다. 나는 재빨리 불빛이 닿지 않는 구석으로 몸을 피했다. 무섭고

full speed. After the first person, two young men came running and panting, who certainly looked like poachers chasing after a baby roe-deer that had escaped the snare.

It so happened that I was sitting in the dark slightly off the shaft of light from the supermarket and therefore off their range of vision. Uncannily still, there was absolutely no one around the supermarket. Often, the number of chairs under the beach parasol was nowhere near enough to seat the usual mob of drinkers, most of whom were construction laborers on their way back home after work. Besides the drinkers, some people from the neighborhood would often sit on those chairs to enjoy the cool night breezes. That night, however, the front yard of the supermarket was completely deserted. In the confusion of the moment, I missed the chance to see the chased person, who had already run into the store. I was able to see the chasing men relatively clearly, though, one in front of the store and the other running into the store.

"Hey you! Bastard! Come out!"

The man wearing red, sleeveless undershirt shouted while running inside. The shirt made his sweat-covered glossy shoulders look enormous.

또 무서웠다. 저렇게 질질 끌려가는 몽달씨를 위해서 내가 해야 할 일이 무엇인지 알 수가 없었다. 도무지 가슴이 떨려 숨도 크게 쉬지 못할 지경이었는데도 김반장은 어질러진 가게를 치우면서 밖은 내다보지도 않았다.

두 명의 사내 중에서도 빨간 셔츠가 훨씬 악독한 게 사실이었다. 녀석은 몽달씨의 머리칼을 한 움큼 휘어 감고서 마치 짐짝을 부리듯 몽달씨를 다루고 있었다. 끌려가지 않으려고 버둥거리다가는 사내의 구둣발에 사정없이 정강이며 옆구리가 뭉개어졌다. 지나가던 행인 몇 사람이 공포에 질린 얼굴로 그들을 지켜보았다. 구경꾼들이 보이자 빨간 셔츠가 당당하게 외쳐 댔다.

"이 새끼, 너 같은 놈은 여지없이 경찰서로 넘겨야 해. 빨리 와!"

불 켜진 강남부동산 앞에서 몽달씨가 최후의 발악을 벌여 놈의 손아귀에서 빠져나왔다. 그러나 이내 녀석에게 머리칼을 붙잡히면서 부동산 옆의 시멘트 기둥에 된통 머리를 받혔다. 쿵. 몽달씨의 머리통이 깨져 나가는 듯한 소리에 나는 눈을 감아 버렸다. 숨이 막힐 것만 같았다. 행복사진관과 원미지물포만 지나고 나면 또다시 불빛도 없는 공터가 나올 것이므로 몽달씨를 구해 낼 시기는 지금

"You'd better come out before we trash the place!"

The other man was still standing in front of the store, huffing and puffing and wiping sweat off his forehead. He was clutching two shirts in one hand. He was also in his undershirt, but his was white and sleeved, which made him look a lot gentler than the man in the red one.

What on earth? My curiosity got the better of me and I peeped in through the door on the side of the store. Perhaps kicked by the chaser, the chased man was already down on the floor on his stomach. Mr. Kim was busy moving the beer boxes around the man in red into the room, shouting something. Just then,

"Brother Kim, Brother Kim, please help me," escaped a faint voice from the fallen man's mouth. Immediately, the man in red stomped on the back of the fallen man.

"You know this piece of shit? Well then, you want the same treatment from us, eh?" yelled the man raising a beer bottle by its neck. Mr. Kim's face turned pale instantly.

"What, what d'you mean? I don't know him! I don't wanna get mixed up in it. It's none of my business. So, whatever you do, do it outside."

밖에 없다. 몽달씨가 악착같이 불 켜진 가게 쪽으로만 몸을 이끌어 갔기 때문에 길 이쪽은 텅 비어 있었다. 몇몇 사람들이 있기는 하였지만 그들은 선불리 끼어들지 않고서 당하는 몽달씨의 처참한 꼴에 혀만 끌끌 차고 있었다.

"빨리 가, 이 자식아! 경찰서로 가잔 말야!"

빨간 셔츠가 움켜쥔 머리칼을 확 낚아채면 몽달씨는 시멘트 바닥에서 몸을 가누지 못해 정말 개처럼 두 손을 바닥에 짚고 끌려갔다.

"왜 이러세요…… 내게 무슨 잘못이…… 있다고……."

행복사진관의 밝은 불빛 앞에서 몽달씨가 울부짖으며 사내에게 잡힌 머리통을 흔들어대다가 녀석의 구둣발에 면상을 짓밟히기 시작하였다. 마침내 나는 내달리기 시작하였다. 두 주먹을 불끈 쥐고 녀석들 곁을 바람같이 스쳐 나는 원미지물포로 뛰어들었다. 가게는 텅 비워 둔 채 지물포 주 씨 아저씨는 아랫목에 길게 누워 텔레비전을 보느라 바깥의 소동은 까맣게 모르고 있었다.

"깡패가, 깡패가 몽달씨를 죽여요."

주 씨 아저씨는 그 우람한 체구에 비하면 말귀를 빨리 알아듣는 사람이었다. 벼락같이 튀어나와 마침 자기 가게 앞을 끌려가고 있는 몽달씨의 꼴을 보고는 냅다 소리를

At the moment, the man who had been writhing on the floor struggled to his feet. Although his face was heavily covered with the blood from his nose, I recognized him. It was none other than Mr. Mongdal. Only then, my eyes began to take in the familiar clothes, which I'd missed when he dashed into the store. It was most definitely Mr. Mongdal in his worn-out pants and his discolored shirt that he always wore under the dyed army jumper.

"You, son of a bitch! What the hell's the matter with you bolting into somebody else's place? Shit like you deserves to be thumped around a bit," the man in red growled baring his white teeth. Suddenly, Mr. Mongdal started to run toward the room where the TV was still blaring. He knew there was another exit through the room. However, a man, faster than Mr. Mongdal, was already there blocking the doorway. It was Mr. Kim.

"Get out! All of you, get out! Take your fight outside and don't ruin my business!"

The red shirt quickly grabbed hold of his victim by the scuff of his neck. Looking at Mr. Mongdal being dragged out like a dog, the white-shirt squirted out spit through his clenched teeth. The eyes of the two drunken men were grotesque with the eerie alco-

질렀다.

“죄가 있으모 경찰을 부를 일이제 무신 일로 사람을 이리 패노? 보소! 형씨, 그 손 못 놓나?”

투박한 경상도 말이 거침없이 쏟아져 나오자 녀석도 약간 주춤했다.

“아저씨는 상관 마쇼! 이런 놈은 경찰서로 끌고 가야 된다구요.”

“누가 뭐라 카노. 야! 빨리 경찰에 신고해라. 당신네들이 사람 뚜드려 가며 경찰서까지 갈 것 없다. 일 분 안에 오토바이 올 테니까.”

“이 아저씨가…… 이 새끼, 아는 사람이오?”

“잘 아는 사람이니 이카제. 이 착한 청년이 무신 죄를 졌다꼬 이래 반 죽여 놨노? 무신 일이라?”

그제야 빨간 셔츠가 슬그머니 움켜쥔 머리칼을 놓았다. 몽달씨가 비틀거리며 주 씨 곁으로 도망쳤다.

“아무 잘못도…… 없어요…… 지나가는 사람 잡아 놓고…… 느닷없이 때리는데.”

더듬더듬, 입안에 괴어 있는 피를 뱉어내며 간신히 이어가는 몽달씨의 말을 듣노라고 주 씨가 잠시 한눈을 판 것이 잘못이었다. 멀찌감치 서서 구경을 하고 있던 사람

holic glint. I quickly shifted away from the light into a dark corner. I was scared, scared to death. I didn't know what to do for Mr. Mongdal who was mercilessly being lugged away. My heart was pounding so hard that I couldn't even breathe properly. Mr. Kim, on the other hand, stayed inside the store, tidying up the clutter; not even once did he care to look out.

It was obvious that the red shirt was more vicious than the other. He grabbed Mr. Mongdal by the hair and manhandled him like a piece of luggage. Struggling to get away, Mr. Mongdal was ruthlessly being kicked on the shin and the side. Some passers-by watched them in horror. Noticing the onlookers, the red shirt shouted undauntedly.

"You, bastard, you should be turned over to the police. Move it!"

In front of the lit window of Kangnam Realtor's, with the last-ditch struggle, Mr. Mongdal managed to get himself free, only to be caught again by the red shirt. Clutching Mr. Mongdal's hair, the red shirt dashed Mr. Mongdal's head against the cement pillar standing next to the realtor's office. I closed my eyes at the loud thud which sounded like Mr. Mongdal's skull caving in. I felt choked. It was the

들 중에서 누군가가 소리쳤다.

"어어. 저 봐요. 저 사람들 도망쳐요!"

정말 눈 깜짝할 사이였다. 벌써 공단 쪽 길로 튕겨 가는 모양으로 발자국 소리만 어지럽고 녀석들은 어둠 속에 파묻혀 버린 뒤였다.

"빨리 가서 잡아야지 저런 놈들 그냥 두면 안 돼요!"

언제 왔는지 김반장이 발을 구르며 흥분하고 있었다. 금방이라도 잡으러 갈 듯 몸을 솟구치는 꼴이 가관이었다.

"소용없어. 저놈들이 어떤 놈이라고."

"세상에, 경찰서로 가자고 그리 당당하게 굴더니 도망치는 것 좀 봐."

"그러니까 그냥 닥치는 대로 골라잡아 팬 거군. 우린 그것도 모르고 정말 도둑이나 되는 줄 알았지 뭐야!"

"여기서 가게들이 많아 환하니깐 어두운 곳으로 끌고 가서 작신 패려고 수작을 벌였군."

"그래요. 아까 보니까 저 윗길에서 이 총각이 그냥 지나가는데 불러 놓고 시비더라구요. 아휴, 저 총각 너무 많이 맞았어. 죽지 않는 게 다행이야."

"그럼 진작에 말하지 그랬어요?"

"누가 이 지경인 줄 알았수? 약국에 가는 길에 그 난리

only chance I had to save Mr. Mongdal since there was a dark empty lot awaiting beyond Happy Photo Studio and Wŏnmi Stationery. Mr. Mongdal was trying his utmost to stick to the side of the street lined with lit stores. On this side of the street there were some people, but not wanting to get rashly involved in the situation, they were just clicking their tongues at the horrible sight of the victim.

"Move it, you bastard! Let's go to the police station!"

Whenever the red shirt yanked at Mr. Mongdal's hair, the poor man couldn't steady himself on his feet and crawled on hands and knees like a dog.

"Why are you doing this to me? What have I done?" cried Mr. Mongdal, in the bright light shedding from Happy Photo Studio, trying to shake his head free in vain, with his hair still in the iron-grip of the red shirt. His questions were answered by the red shirt stamping down on his face. Finally, I broke into a run. Hands clenched, I flew past them into Wŏnmi Stationery. The shop was left untended and the shop owner, Mr. Chu was watching TV lying down deep inside the room, completely oblivious to the trouble outside his shop.

"Some hoodlums are trying to kill Mr. Mongdal!"

길래 무서워서 저쪽으로 돌아갔다가 약 사 갖고 와 보니 경찰서 가자고 여태도 패고 있던걸.”

모여 섰던 사람들이 저마다 한마디씩 떠들어대기 시작했다. 조금 아까까지도 텅 비어 있다시피 한 거리였는데 언제 알았는지 이 집 저 집에서 쏟아져 나온 사람들이 웅성거리며 피투성이가 된 몽달씨를 기웃거렸다. 참말이지 쥐어뜯긴 머리칼하며 길바닥을 쓸고 온 옷 꼬락서니, 그리고 피범벅이 된 얼굴까지가 영락없이 몽달귀신 그대로였다.

“무신 놈의 세상이 이리 험악하노. 이래가꼬는 사람이라 할 수 있겠나?”

주 씨가 어이없어 하는데 또 김반장이 냉큼 뛰어들었다.

“그러게 말입니다. 하여간 저놈들을 잡아 넘겼어야 하는 건데…… 좀 어때? 대체 이게 무슨 꼴인가. 어서 집으로 가세. 내가 데려다 줄게.”

김반장이 몽달씨를 부축해 일으켰다. 세상에 밸도 없지, 그 손을 뿌리치지 못하고 몽달씨는 김반장의 부축을 받으며 집으로 갔다.

몽달씨를 다시 보게 된 것은 그로부터 꼭 열흘이 지난 며칠 전이었다. 그 열흘간을 어떻게 보냈는지는 설명하기

Despite his enormous size, he was quick-witted. He ran out at lightning speed and, at the sight of Mr. Mongdal being lugged in front of his shop, he shouted at the top of his lungs,

"If he's guilty, shouldn't you call the police? Why are you beating him? Look here, let him go, will ya?"

The red shirt was a bit taken aback at the crude Kyongsang dialect pouring out of Mr. Chu's mouth.

"Mister, it's no concern of yours! Scum like this should be hauled to the police."

"No objection there. Hey, call the police quickly. You don't need to beat him up all the way to the police station. Police motorbikes will be here in a minute."

"Look, Mister! You know this bastard?"

"Of course, I know him. That's what I mean. What has this nice young man done to deserve such a horrible beating. You've half killed him. What has he done, anyway?"

Only then, the red shirt slowly let go of Mr. Mongdal's hair. Mr. Mongdal staggered to Mr. Chu.

"I... haven't done anything... wrong... was just passing by... they suddenly grabbed me... started beating me for no reason."

도 귀찮을 정도였다. 몽달씨와 더불어 다닐 때는 몰랐지만 막상 그가 없으니 심심해서 미칠 지경이었다. 하루가 꼭 마흔 시간쯤으로 늘어난 느낌이었다. 때때로는 형제슈퍼의 의자에 앉아 있은 적도 있었지만 이미 김반장과는 서먹한 사이가 되어 버려서 그다지 자주 찾지는 않았다. 그날 밤, 내가 몰래 가게 안을 훔쳐보고 있는 줄을 모르는 김반장만큼은 예전과 다름없이 굴고 있기는 하였다.

"경옥이 처제. 요새는 왜 뜸해? 선옥이 언니 서울서 오거든 직방으로 내게 알리는 것 잊지 마. 그러면 내가 이것 주지!"

김반장이 쳐들어 보이는 것은 으레 요깡이었다. 껍질에는 영양갱이라고 씌어 있는 이백 원짜리 팥떡인데, 그것을 죽자 사자 먹고 싶어 하는 것을 아는 까닭이었다. 그러나 흥, 어림도 없지. 선옥이 언니가 오게 되면 김반장의 비겁한 행동을 미주알고주알 일러바쳐서 행여 남아 있을지도 모를 미련까지도 아예 싹둑 끊어 버리게 하자는 것이 내 속셈이었다. 어찌 된 셈인지 선옥이 언니는 한 달 가까이 집에는 코빼기도 내비치지 않고 있었다. 얼마 전에 서울에 다녀온 엄마 말로는 양품점이 한 달에 두 번 노는데도 집에 올 생각 않고 온종일 쏘다니다 밤늦게야 기

Haltingly, Mr. Mongdal talked, spitting blood out of his mouth all the while. Unfortunately, Mr. Chu was briefly distracted from the two hoodlums while listening to Mr. Mongdal. One of the onlookers standing at a distance yelled,

"Hey, look! They're getting away!"

It happened in a wink. By the time we looked in the direction, they'd already disappeared into darkness; but we heard their hasty footsteps coming from the direction of the industrial complex.

"We've got to go after them quick. We can't let those bastards get away!"

Mr. Kim—God only knows when he showed up there—shouted indignantly, stamping and heaving his chest as if he were about to set out in pursuit of the hooligans; he was quite a sight to see.

"It's useless. We're no match for the kind."

"What in the world! Look at them run! What's happened to their righteous talk about taking him to the police?"

"It's obvious now. They just picked whoever came their way and started whacking him. We were completely duped. We thought he was a thief or something."

"It's bright here with the light from the stores, so

어들어 온다는 것이었다. 게다가 이모가 받아 본 전화 속의 남자들만도 서넛이 넘어서 양품점 전화통이 종일토록 불나게 울려대는 바람에 지깐년은 저한테 걸려오는 전화 받기에도 바쁜 형편이라 했다. 엄마를 쏙 빼닮아 말뽄새가 거칠기 짝이 없는 이모가 보나마나 바가지로 퍼부었을 선옥이 언니의 흉보따리를 잔뜩 짊어지고 온 엄마의 마지막 결론은 갈데없이 원미동 똑똑이다웠다.

"선옥이 고년, 이왕지사 바람 든 년이니까 차라리 탈렌트나 영화배우를 시키는 게 낫겠습디다. 말이사 바른 말이지 인물이야 요즘 헌다 하는 장미희보다 낫지……."

"미쳤군, 미쳤어. 탈렌트는 누가 거저 시켜 주남. 뜨신 밥 먹고 식은 소리 작작 해!"

그렇게 몰아붙이면서도 아버지는 으레 흐흐흐 웃고 마는 게 예사였다. 딸 많은 집구석에 인물 팔아 돈 버는 딸년 하나쯤 생긴다 해서 나쁠 것도 없다는 웃음이 분명했다.

"서울 사람들은 눈도 밝지. 선옥이가 명동으로 나갔다 하면 영화배우 해 보라고 줄줄이 따라다닌답니다. 인물 좋은 것도 딱 귀찮다고 고년이 어찌 성가셔 하는지……."

엄마도 참, 입술에 침도 안 바르고 고흥댁 아줌마한테 이렇게 주워섬기는 때도 있었다. 그러면 여태도 동아 언

they were taking him to some place dark to beat him to their fill."

"You're right. I saw them on the street up there. This young man was just passing by when they stopped him and tried to pick a quarrel with him. Dear me! He's got a good beating, hasn't he? It's a miracle he's survived."

"Why didn't you say so, then?"

"I had no idea that it would turn this bad. I saw the trouble on my way to the drugstore, so I took a different route. Coming back, I saw them still beating him, threatening to take him to the police."

Everybody began to say something. The street was almost empty up until a few minutes before, but now crowded with people pouring out of their houses all around. I couldn't figure out how they learned of the incident. They were all talking and craning their necks to see Mr. Mongdal, who looked true to his nickname, hair pulled out, clothes caked with dirt, and face covered with blood.

"What's the world coming to? So mean and evil, are they really human?" said Mr. Chu shaking his head in despair. Hearing him, Mr. Kim quickly responded,

"That's what I'm saying. We should have caught

니 콧대가 하늘 높은 줄 모르고 솟아 있다고만 믿는 고흥댁 아주머니도 지지 않고 딸 자랑을 쏟아 놓았다.

"우리 동아는 요새 피아노도 배우고 꽃꽂이 학원도 다닌다고 맨날 바쁘다요. 시방 세상은 그 정도의 신부 수업인가 뭔가가 아주 필수라 한다드만."

엄마도 엄마지만 고흥댁 아주머니 말은 듣기에 거북하였다. 대신설비 노가다 청년한테 시집가면 피아노는커녕, 호박꽃 한 송이 꽂을 일도 없을 것이니까. 어른들은 알고 보면 하나밖에 모르는 멍텅구리 같을 때가 종종 있는 법이다. 그 사건 이후, 김반장에 대한 이야기만 해도 그렇다.

"김반장 그 사람 참말이제 진국은 진국인기라. 엊그제만 해도 복숭아 깡통 하나 들고 몽달 청년한테 갔능갑드라. 걱정도 억시기 해쌌고, 우찌 됐건 미친놈한테 그만큼 정성 들이는 것만 봐도 보통은 아닌 기 맞다."

지물포 주 씨가 행복사진관 엄 씨한테 하는 말이었다. 세 살 많다 하여 어김없이 형님으로 받드는 엄 씨가 고개를 끄덕이며 맞장구치는 것을 보고 있으면 내 속이 터질 것만 같았다. 그렇지만 이상하게도 그 밤의 일을 속 시원히 털어놓을 수가 없었다. 그러고 보면 이 김경옥이야말로 진국 중에 진국인지도 모른다.

and turned them over to the police! Are you okay? My god, look at you! Let's go home, I'll take you home."

Mr. Kim helped Mr. Mongdal to his feet. 'Doesn't he ever get disgusted or offended?' He simply returned home with Mr. Kim that night.

It was several days ago, ten days after the incident, to be exact, when I saw Mr. Mongdal again. I can't even begin to talk about how I spent those ten days. I had no idea how boring it could be without Mr. Mongdal while hanging out with him, but once he wasn't there with me any longer, I nearly died of boredom. I felt that the number of hours a day somehow increased to forty. I tried sitting on a chair in front of Brothers Supermarket, but I rarely did it since I felt like keeping a distance from Mr. Kim. Ignorant of the fact that I witnessed what had happened inside the store that night, Mr. Kim behaved as always.

"Kyŏng-ok, my sister-in-law. What's the matter? You don't come here as often. When your sister comes down from Seoul, don't forget to tell me as soon as possible. Then, you'll get one of these!"

In his raised hand, I saw a bar of sweet red-bean paste, as usual. He knew that was my favorite and I

몽달씨가 자리 털고 일어난 이야기를 하려다가 또 다른 쪽으로 새 버렸지만 몽달씨야말로 진짜 이상한 사람이었다. 오후반인 소라가 등교 준비를 해야 한다고 서둘러 저희 집으로 가 버린 때니까 정오가 조금 지나서였을 것이다. 집으로 가다 말고 문득 형제슈퍼 쪽을 돌아보니 음료수 박스들을 차곡차곡 쟁여 놓는 일에 땀을 뻘뻘 흘리고 있는 몽달씨가 보였다. 실컷 두들겨 맞고 열흘간이나 누워 있었던 사람이라 안색이 차마 마주 보기 어려울 만큼 핼쑥했다. 그런데도 뭐가 좋은지 히죽히죽 웃어 가면서 열심히 박스들을 나르고 있는 게 아닌가. 그것도 김반장네 가게에서. 아무리 눈을 크게 뜨고 보아도 몽달씨가 분명했다. 저럴 수가. 어쨌든 제정신이 아닌 작자임이 틀림없었다. 아무리 정신이 좀 헷갈린 사람이래도 그렇지, 그날 밤의 김반장 행동을 깡그리 잊어버리지 않고서야 저럴 수가 없다는 게 내 생각이었다.

잊었을까. 그날 밤 머리의 어딘가를 세게 다쳐서 김반장이 자기를 내쫓은 부분만큼만 감쪽같이 지워진 것은 아닐까. 전혀 엉뚱한 이야기만도 아니었다. 텔레비전에서도 보면 기억상실증인가 뭔가로 자기 아들도 못 알아보는 연속극이 있었다. 그런 쪽의 상상이라면 나를 따라올 만한

would do almost anything to have one. Humph, go ahead, dream on, Mr. Kim!' I had a plan: as soon as Sŏn-ok came home, I would tell her everything about Mr. Kim's coward behavior, down to the smallest detail. My plan was to nip in the bud any possible lingering feelings in my sister's heart toward Mr. Kim. For some reason, however, we'd seen nothing of Sŏn-ok for about a month. According to my mother, who had been to Seoul some time ago, my sister never even dreamed of coming home even on her off-duty days twice a month. On those off-duty days, she spent the whole day wandering all over the city, returning to Aunt's only late at night. Moreover, my aunt was getting phone calls from three or four different men asking for Sŏn-ok. The phone at the clothes store was ringing off the hook all day long and "that wretched girl" was much too busy answering the calls from men. My aunt, who is neck and neck with my mother when it comes to the use of rough language, must have poured out to my mother all the faults she'd found with my sister. Despite the sheer weight on her mind of what she'd heard about her daughter from her sister, my mother's final conclusion was worthy of her nickname, the town's brain,

아이가 없는 형편이었다. 내 머릿속은 기기괴괴한 온갖 상상들로 늘 모래주머니처럼 빽빽했으니까. 나는 청소부 아버지의 딸이 아니라 사실은 어느 부잣집의 버려진 딸이다, 라는 식의 유치한 상상은 작년도 못 되어 이미 졸업했었다. 요즘의 내 상상이란 외계인 아버지와 지구인 엄마와의 사랑, 뭐 그런 쪽의 의젓한 것이었다. 아무튼 나의 기막힌 상상력으로 인해 몽달씨는 부분적인 기억상실증 환자로 결정되었다. 그렇다면 이제는 확인할 일만 남은 셈이다. 오래 기다릴 필요도 없었다. 나는 김반장네 가게 일을 거들어 주고 난 뒤 비치파라솔 밑의 의자에 앉아 뭔가를 읽고 있는 몽달씨에게 갔다. 보나마나 주머니 속에 잔뜩 들어 있는 종잇조각 중의 하나일 것이었다. 멀쩡한 정신도 아닌 주제에 이번엔 기억상실증이란 병까지 얻어 놓고도 여태 시 따위나 읽고 있는 몽달씨 꼴이 한심했다.

"이거, 또 시예요?"

"그래. 슬픈 시야. 아주 슬픈……."

몽달씨가 핼쑥한 얼굴을 쳐들며 행복하게 웃었다. 슬픈 시라고 해 놓고서 웃다니. 나는 이맛살을 찡그리며 몽달씨 옆에 앉았다. 그리고 아주 낮은 목소리로 물었다.

"이제 다 나았어요?"

"Sŏn-ok, that wench of a girl! She's already gone foul, so she had best become a TV talent or an actress. Frankly speaking, when it comes to good looks, she's better than the famous Chang Mi-hŭi."

"Have you gone mad? You figure it's easy to become a talent? Stop talking nonsense!"

While ruthlessly berating my mother, my father, as usual, ended up laughing contentedly under his breath. The laughter obviously meant to say nothing was wrong with having a daughter, among so many girls in the family, who would make money by taking advantage of her good looks.

"Seoulites have an eye for pretty girls. Whenever Sŏn-ok turns up in Myŏng-dong, downtown, files of people follow her, asking if she's interested in becoming an actress. She keeps complaining it's such a nuisance to have good looks."

My mother once rattled away to Madam Kohŭng. Still believing in her daughter's great ambition, Madam Kohŭng struck back with a series of her daughter's praises:

"My Tong-a has been so busy what with piano lessons and flower arrangement classes. These days, that kind of bridal lessons are a must, they say."

Aside from my mother, Madam Kohŭng's remarks

"응. 시를 읽으면서 누워 있었더니 금방 나왔지."

금방은 무슨 금방. 열흘이나 되었는데. 또 한 번 나는 몽달씨의 형편없는 정신 상태에 실망했다.

"그날 밤에 난 여기에 앉아서 다 봤어요."

"무얼?"

"김반장이 아저씨를 쫓아내는 것……."

순간 몽달씨가 정색을 하고 내 얼굴을 쳐다보았다. 예전의 그 풀려 있던 눈동자가 아니었다. 까맣고 반짝이는 눈이었다. 그러나 잠깐이었다. 다시는 내 얼굴을 보지 않을 작정인지 괜스레 팔뚝에 엉겨 붙은 상처 딱지를 떼어내려고 애쓰는 척했다. 나는 더욱 바싹 다가앉았다.

"김반장은 나쁜 사람이야. 그렇지요?"

몽달씨가 팔뚝을 탁 치면서 "아니야"라고 응수했는데도 나는 계속 다그쳤다.

"그렇지요? 맞죠?"

그래도 몽달씨는 못 들은 척 팔뚝만 문지르고 있었다. 바보같이. 기억상실도 아니면서…… 나는 자꾸만 약이 올라 견딜 수 없는데도 몽달씨는 마냥 딴전만 피우고 있었다.

"슬픈 시가 있어. 들어 볼래?"

made me ill at ease. If Tong-a married the part-time laborer, she would never have a chance to arrange even a stem of pumpkin flower, let alone play the piano. Once you know well enough how the minds of grown-ups work, you get to see how stupid they can be at times with their tunnel vision and all. The same thing applies to what Mr. Kim did after the incident.

"Mr. Kim's truly the salt of the earth. Couple of days back, people saw him on his way to that young man, Mongdal, carrying a can of peach. He's been worried sick about the poor man. Watching him putting so much in tending the crazy man, I must say Mr. Kim's not an ordinary man," said Mr. Chu, owner of Paper Shop, to Mr. Ŏm, owner of Happy Photo Studio. Watching Mr. Ŏm—three years senior to and therefore always treated with due respect by Mr. Chu—nodding in response, my heart was about to explode, full of resentment. Nevertheless, for some reason, I couldn't bring myself to take it all out of my chest to somebody. From that angle, I, Kim Kyŏng-ok, may well be the salt of 'the salt of the earth.'

I've digressed again, when in fact I want to talk about Mr. Mongdal after the incident. I can't empha-

치, 누가 그 따위 시를 듣고 싶어 할 줄 알고 내가 입술을 비죽 내밀거나 말거나 몽달씨는 기어이 시를 읊고 있었다. ……마른 가지로 자기 몸과 마음에 바람을 들이는 저 은사시나무는, 박해받는 순교자 같다. 그러나 다시 보면 저 은사시나무는 박해받고 싶어 하는 순교자 같다…….

"너 글씨 알지? 자, 이것 가져. 나는 다 외웠으니까."

몽달씨가 구깃구깃한 종이쪽지를 내게로 내밀었다. 아주 슬픈 시라고 말하면서. 시는 전혀 슬픈 것 같지 않았는데도 난 자꾸만 눈물이 나려 하였다. 바보같이, 다 알고 있었으면서…… 바보 같은 몽달씨…….

(소설 속에 인용된 시는 순서대로 김정환, 이하석, 황지우 씨의 작품임.)

『원미동 사람들』, 살림, 2004(1986)

size enough how strange a man Mr. Mongdal's turned out to be. It was when So-ra hurried back home saying that she had to prepare for her afternoon school, so it must have been slightly after noon. Walking toward home, I turned a quick glance at the supermarket and found Mr. Mongdal busy carefully stacking up the beverage boxes, sweating profusely. After ten days in bed recovering from the injuries inflicted by the horrendous beating, he looked so sallow that I couldn't even look him directly in the eye. To my amazement, however, he was diligently carrying the boxes, with a happy grin around his mouth, at Mr. Kim's supermarket, for God's sake! I stared at him with my eyes wide open, in case I mistook someone else for him, but he was really Mr. Mongdal himself. I couldn't believe my eyes. 'He must be an insane person indeed,' I thought. Still, even if he was a little bit beside himself, how could he do a thing like that, unless he'd forgotten all about Mr. Kim's behavior on the night of the incident?

'Has he really forgotten? Perhaps, he had his head dashed against something so hard that he lost his memory, perhaps only the part where Mr. Kim kicked him out of the supermarket,' which is not a completely unprecedented thing. There was a TV soap opera in which a mother couldn't even recognize her own son for something called amnesia or other. When it comes to imagination of that sort, no child can beat me; my head is packed to capacity like a sand bag with all kinds of weird imaginations. The scenario in which I'm not a daughter of a garbage man, but an abandoned daughter of a rich family has already become outdated couple of years ago. Recently, new scenarios center on something like the love between an extraterrestrial father and an earth mother, much more sophisticated than before! Anyway, my amazing power of imagination diagnosed Mr. Mongdal's case as amnesia. Now, all I had left to do is confirm the diagnosis. There was no need to wait, so I walked up to Mr. Mongdal who, finished with all the chores at the store, was reading something, sitting on a chair under the beach parasol. I didn't need to see what he was reading; most likely, it was one of the folded papers he always carried in his pockets. He looked utterly pathetic, now that he'd got amnesia added to his already existing condition of insanity.

"Is it a poem, again?"

"Yes, it's a sad poem. Very sad."

Mr. Mongdal turned up his pale face to meet my eyes and smiled happily. He said it was a sad poem, yet he smiled! Furrowing my forehead, I sat next to him and asked him in a very soft voice,

"Are you okay now?"

"Yes, I quickly got better while reading poems in bed."

What was so quick about it? It was as long as ten days. Once more, I got bitterly disappointed at Mr. Mongdal's poor mental state.

"On that night, I sat here and saw everything."

"What did you see?"

"Mr. Kim was driving you out of his store."

Suddenly, he stared at me with a serious look in his eyes. They were not the usual unfocused eyes of his; instead, they were pitch black and sparkling. However, it was only for a brief moment. He cast his eyes down, perhaps determined not to look at my face again, at a scab clotted and dried on his forearm and pretended to try peeling the scab off. I moved closer to him,

"Mr. Kim is bad, isn't he?"

Mr. Mongdal said, "No!" patting himself on the forearm. I was not to back down,

"Isn't he? I'm right, aren't I?"

Mr. Mongdal kept rubbing his forearm, pretending he didn't hear me. 'Silly Mr. Mongdal! You've never lost your memory!' I could hardly suppress my anger, yet Mr. Mongdal pretended not to notice it.

"I've got a sad poem here. You want to hear it?"

'Big deal! Who ever wants to listen to things like poems?' Paying no attention to my pouted lips, he started reciting the poem anyway. "Letting the wind into its body and mind through withered limbs, the poplar tree yonder looks like a martyr being persecuted; then again, the poplar tree looks like a martyr wanting to be persecuted."

"You can read, can't you? Take it, it's yours. I've already memorized it."

He pushed the crumpled paper toward me, repeating it was a very sad poem. Though it didn't sound like a sad poem at all, I felt like crying. 'Silly you! You remember everything. Silly Mr. Mongdal!'

(The poets quoted in the story are Kim Chŏng-hwan, Yi Ha-sŏk, and Hwang Ji-woo in order.)

Translated by Jeon Miseli

해설
Afterword

폭력의 시대, 시인은 노래한다

정영훈(문학평론가)

양귀자의 소설 「원미동 시인」(1986)은 『원미동 사람들』(1992) 연작에 포함된 작품 가운데 하나다. 『원미동 사람들』 연작의 공간적 배경은 부천시 원미동으로, 부천의 지정학적 위상은 『원미동 사람들』 연작을 이해하는 데 중요한 역할을 한다. 『원미동 사람들』 연작의 첫 번째 작품인 「멀고 아름다운 동네」(1986)가 잘 보여 주고 있듯이, 부천은 서울이라는 중심부와 경계를 맞대고 있는 주변, 서울로 진입하지 못했거나 서울에서 밀려난 사람들이 여러 가지 복잡한 심정을 안고서 서울과 관계하며 살아가고 있는 곳이다. 서울 바깥에 산다는 사실로써 자기를 규정하고 있다는 점에서 이곳 사람들은 스스로를 타자로 여기는 사

A Violent Time, A Poet Sings

Jeong Yong-hoon (literary critic)

"The Poet of Wŏnmi-dong" (1986), a short story by Yang Kwi-ja, is one of the stories included in *The People of Wŏnmi-dong* (1992), a series set in the Wŏnmi-dong neighborhood of the city of Puch'ŏn. It is critical for readers to grasp Puch'ŏn's geopolitical status in order to understand these stories. As the opening tale "The Faraway Beautiful Neighborhood" (1986) vividly illustrates, Puch'ŏn is a peripheral place on the outskirts of Seoul, a place where those who haven't yet made it to Seoul as the center, or who were pushed out from it, live with a complex set of various emotions and in some relation to Seoul. It can be safely assumed, since the characters

람들이라 할 수 있다. 「원미동 시인」에도 이런 정서가 밑바탕에 깔려 있다.

「원미동 시인」은 일곱 살짜리 어린아이를 화자로 내세워 이야기를 풀어 간다. 어린아이를 화자로 내세운 소설들이 대개 그렇듯이 소설은 어른들의 세계가 애써 감춰두고 싶어 하는 것들을 들추어낸다. 마치 세상 이치를 다 알고 있다는 듯이 행동하는, 조금은 영악하고 또 그만큼 순진하기도 한 아이의 눈에는 어른들의 세계가 어수룩하고 속물적으로 보인다. 아이는 김반장이 자기를 살갑게 대하는 이유가 무엇인지, 김반장과 언니가 맺어질 가능성이 얼마나 낮은지 환하게 알고, 딸이 '노가다 청년'과 죽고 못 사는 사이라는 사실을 모른 채 유세를 떨어대는 고흥댁 아주머니를 비웃는가 하면, 언니들의 삶이 바라는 만큼 그렇게 순탄하게 전개되지 않으리라는 것도 눈치채고 있다.

그런데 이런 아이의 눈으로 보기에도 조금 낯선 인물이 하나 있다. '원미동 시인'이라고도 하고 '몽달씨'라고도 하는 청년이다. 청년에게 이런 별명이 붙은 것은 그가 조금 모자라는 듯이 행동하는 데다 언제나 중얼중얼 시를 외우고 다니기 때문이다. 동네 사람들의 말로 그는 대학까지

define themselves by the fact that they reside outside Seoul, that they also identify themselves as outsiders, or the Other. This sensibility forms the undercurrent of "The Poet of Wŏnmi-dong."

The story is told through the eyes of a seven-year-old girl. As is often the case in fiction with a child narrator, what is revealed is what the adult world goes to great lengths to keep hidden. To a child, a bit clever but just as innocent, who behaves as if she knows how things ought to be, the world of adults looks naive and snobby. She sees through the sweetness shown to her by Mr. Kim, the neighborhood supervisor; knows that a union between her older sister and Mr. Kim is highly unlikely; laughs at Mrs. Kohŭng who crows about her daughter, unaware that she is madly in love with a "redneck chap"; and also suspects that the road her older sisters will travel won't be as smooth as they wish.

But there is one person who is hard to figure out even for this keen-eyed child: a young man called either "poet from Wŏnmi-dong" or "Mr. Mongdal." His nickname stems from his somewhat odd mannerisms and constant mumbling of poems. According to neighbors, he was expelled from col-

다녔는데 데모를 하다 제적을 당했고 곧장 군대에 끌려간 후 사람이 이상해졌다 한다. 소설이 드러내 놓고 이야기를 하고 있지는 않지만, 청년이 겪은 일련의 일은 1980년대 초반 한국의 정치적 역사적 현실과 큰 관련이 있다. 그 당시 쿠데타로 정권을 잡은 군인들은 민주화를 바라는 사람들의 열망을 묵살하고 힘으로 이들을 제압했다. 당연히 반발이 있었고, 그 과정에서 수많은 대학생들이 데모를 하다 제적을 당하거나 강제로 군대에 징집당했다. 소설 속 청년이 그랬던 것처럼 말이다.

소설은 이런 현실을 직접 비판하는 대신 다소 우화적인 삽화를 통해 이를 드러낸다. 어느 초여름 밤, 아이는 엄마와 아버지의 말다툼이 급기야 험악한 욕설과 아버지의 손찌검으로 이어지는 걸 보다 슬그머니 집을 나와 김반장의 가게로 온다. 거기서 아이는 몽달씨가 웬 깡패들에게 얻어맞는 장면을 목격한다. 이해할 수 없는 것은 김반장과 동네 사람들의 태도였다. 몽달씨는 사람들에게서 도망쳐 김반장의 가게로 들어갔는데, 김반장은 자기에게 불똥이 튈까 봐 몽달씨를 외면하고 모른 척했고, 동네 사람들 역시 선뜻 나서서 몽달씨를 구해 주려 하지 않았다. 그러다 지물포 주 씨 아저씨가 나서 사태가 해결되자 그제야 한

lege for participating in demonstrations and then immediately drafted. He has been unbalanced ever since, they say. Though it is never spelled out in the story, the events that the young man experienced have much to do with the political and historical conditions of the early 1980s in South Korea. In those days, the military junta that took power in a coup d'état paid no heed to people's aspiration for democracy and ruled them with brute force. In the ensuing pushback, many college students took to the streets in mass demonstrations, and many were subsequently thrown out of school and or immediately drafted, exactly like the young man in the story.

Instead of directly criticizing this reality, the novel reveals it through more or less allegorical episodes. One early summer night, the child watches her mother and father arguing, and then exchanging ugly epithets, which eventually leads to her father physically attacking her mother. At that point, the girl slips out of the house and heads to Mr. Kim's corner store. On the way, she stumbles upon a scene where Mr. Mongdal is being beaten up by some gang members. What baffles her is the way Mr. Kim and other neighbors respond. When Mr.

마디씩 말을 보태며 몽달씨에게 동정을 표하는 것이 아닌가. 아이는 어른들의 이런 태도를 도무지 이해할 수가 없다. 마치 그런 일이 없었다는 듯 몽달씨를 대하는 김반장의 태도에 어이가 없어 하기도 한다. 동네 사람들과 김반장의 태도는 현실 정치의 폭력 앞에서 아무 항변도 하지 못하고 자기의 안전만을 생각한 채 몸을 움츠리고 살아가는 소시민들의 모습을 떠올리게 한다. 소설은 어린아이의 눈을 통해 이를 고발하고 있는 것이다.

며칠 후 아이는 몽달씨가 땀을 흘려 가며 김반장의 일을 도와주는 모습을 보고 의아해한다. 김반장의 행동을 깡그리 잊어버리지 않고서야 그럴 수 없다고 생각한 까닭이다. 답답한 마음에 아이는 몽달씨에게 그날 있었던 일을 다 지켜보고 있었다고 고백하며, 김반장은 나쁜 사람이라고 비난한다. 그러나 몽달씨는 아이의 이야기를 외면한다. 몽달씨는 그때의 기억을 잃어버린 것이 아니라 짐짓 그런 척하고 있는 것일 뿐이었다. 몽달씨는 대신 아이에게 어느 시인(황지우)의 시를 읊어 준다. “마른 가지로 자기 몸과 마음에 바람을 들이는 저 은사시나무는, 박해받는 순교자 같다. 그러나 다시 보면 저 은사시나무는 박해 받고 싶어 하는 순교자 같다” 하고. 몽달씨는 자기를

Mongdal manages to break away from the gangsters and run into Mr. Kim's store, Mr. Kim turns away, pretending to be oblivious so as not to get involved, and the neighbors don't step forward to help Mr. Mongdal either. Only after Mr. Chu, who owns the neighborhood paper goods store, happens to show up and resolves the situation do the others express their sympathy to Mr. Mongdal in a few words. To the child, the attitude of the adults is utterly incomprehensible. That Mr. Kim treats Mr. Mongdal as if nothing had happened leaves the little girl speechless. The attitude of the neighbors and Mr. Kim alludes to that of ordinary citizens of the petty bourgeois class who keep quiet in the face of ongoing political violence and cower in fear for their own safety. Yang's fiction is an indictment of this attitude through a child's eyes.

Several days later, the child is surprised that Mr. Mongdal breaks a sweat helping Mr. Kim with his work. This seems implausible to her unless Mr. Mongdal has completely forgotten how Mr. Kim treated him just days before. Out of frustration, she confesses to Mr. Mongdal that she saw the entire episode that day and criticizes Mr. Kim as a bad person. However, Mr. Mongdal turns away, deflect-

박해 받고 싶어 하는 순교자로 여기고 있는지도 모른다. 몽달씨가 순교자의 마음으로 사람들에게 알려주고 싶어 했던 것은 아마도 우리 모두가 박해자라는 사실이 아니었을까. 폭력에 맞서지 못하는 사람들은 크든 작든 폭력에 가담하고 있는 것이라고, 그러니 그들 역시 가해자라고 이야기하고 싶었던 것이 아닐까.

ing her words. He hasn't forgotten what happened; he is only pretending to. Instead, Mr. Mongdal recites a poem by poet Hwang Ji-woo to the child.

"Letting the wind into its body and mind through withered limbs, the poplar tree yonder looks like a martyr being persecuted; then again, the poplar tree looks like a martyr wanting to be persecuted."

Perhaps Mr. Mongdal considers himself a martyr who longs to be persecuted. Maybe, in a martyr's frame of mind, he wants to send us the message that we are all persecutors. He may be trying to say that, if you are not standing up to violence, you are in fact participating in that violence, which makes you a perpetrator.

비평의 목소리

Critical Acclaim

양귀자가 그려 보이는 원미동은 작고도 큰 세계이다. 그 세계는 소설 속에서는 부천시 원미동이라는 구체적 장소에서, 그 장소에 살고 있는 몇몇 인물들이 펼쳐 보이는 작은 삶들로 이루어져 있지만, 양귀자의 소설을 읽는 독자들에게 그 세계는 커다란 세계이다. 그것은 원미동의 세계가 지금 우리가 살고 있는 삶이기 때문이다. 부천·부평·주안·시흥·안양·군포, 그리고 서울 변두리의 고만고만한 동네에서 우리는 원미동을 만난다. 원미동은 '멀고 아름다운 동네'라는 문자 그대로의 의미로, 양귀자의 역설적 표현을 빌면 '가나안에서 무릉도원까지'의 아득한 거리에 있는 동네가 아니라, '기어이 또 하나의 희망'을 만들

The Wŏnmi-dong that Yang Kwi-ja portrays is a world both small and large. The world in the novel is a specific place with a particular name, Wŏnmi-dong, Puch'ŏn City, populated by a handful of characters who live small and insignificant lives. But to us, Yang's readers, that world is a big one, because Wŏnmi-dong includes the world we all live in right now. In Puch'ŏn, Pup'yŏng, Chuan, Sihŭng, Anyang, Kunp'o, and other similar towns and neighborhoods all around Seoul, we meet Wŏnmi-dong. Though the name Wŏnmi-dong literally means "a faraway, beautiful neighborhood," it is not as "far away as Canaan is from the Peach-Blossomed Paradise" as in

어 가며 살아야 할 우리들의 동네이다. 그러므로 원미동은 작고도 큰 세계이다.

홍정선

양귀자는 현대 사회에 만연한 다양한 폭력의 징후들을 감내하며 힘겹게 살아가는 소시민들의 삶을 따스한 어조로 그려낸다. 절망의 나락에서 고통을 무화시키는 희망의 불씨를 피워 낸다. (중략) 「원미동 시인」 역시 폭력 문제를 다루고 있다. 자신에게 가해진 폭력과 위선을 고스란히 감내하면서 스스로 박해 받는 순교자이기를 원하는 몽달 씨의 모습은 마치 간디의 무저항주의나, 십자가에 매달린 예수의 모습을 떠올리게 한다. 이처럼 박해 받는 순교자의 이미지는 인간의 무력함을 인간의 위대함으로 바꾸는 방식, 다시 말해 인간의 나약함을 폭력에 대한 하나의 도덕적 상징의 자리로 끌어올리는 방식이라고 할 수 있다. 특히 작가는 끊임없이 시를 웅얼거리는 몽달 씨의 모습을 통해, 폭력에 대해 현실적으로는 무력하지만, 도덕적으로는 폭력과 맞서는 가장 순결한 상징인 문학에 대한 자신의 인식을 투영하고 있다.

그러나 작가는 폭력의 징후들로 가득 찬 세계에서 살아

the author's paradoxical expression in the story, but it is our own neighborhood in which we have no choice but to live "determined to build one more dream somehow." Thus Wŏnmi-dong is at once a small place and a big one.

Hong Jeong-sun

Yang Kwi-ja warmly portrays the difficult lives of ordinary people who have to endure various manifestations of the violence pervasive in modern society. Out of the abyss of despair, she conjures up a seed of hope to soothe the pain. (omission) "The Poet of Wŏnmi-dong" also deals with the violence. The image of Mr. Mongdal, who embraces the aggression and hypocrisy directed toward him and chooses to be a persecuted martyr, has striking affinities with Gandhi, who advocated non-violent resistance, and Jesus on the cross. Thus the imagery of a martyr turns human powerlessness into human strength, elevating human vulnerability to the height of moral symbolism in opposing violence. In particular, the author is projecting onto Mr. Mongdal's incessant mumbling of poems her own understanding of literature as the purest symbolic weapon in the moral fight against violence despite literature's

가는 사람들의 암울한 삶을 그려 내면서도 그 속에서 어떤 희망의 불씨를 찾으려고 노력한다. 작가가 작중 인물들이 보여 주는 어리석음과 무능함, 얄팍한 이해타산이나 자질구레한 이기적 욕망들, 혹은 이웃들이 겪는 부당한 폭력에 무관심한 그들의 비겁함과 소심함까지도 감싸 안는 것은 작가가 끝까지 인간에 대한 희망을 버리지 않았음을 반증한다. 한없이 스산하고 누추한 이들의 삶을 감싸고 있는 작가의 따뜻한 시선이 바로 작가가 지피는 희망의 불씨, 우리에게 전해 주는 온기인 것이다.

박혜경

existential helplessness in the face of that violence. At the same time, while chronicling the discouraging lives people lead in a world suffused with violence, the author never stops searching that bleak reality for some spark, some reason for hope. Despite the folly and incompetence of her characters, the shallow calculations they make and the sundry selfish desires they harbor, and even the cowardice and pettiness of those who are indifferent to their neighbor's suffering from violence, the author hugs them all, hinting that she has never given up on humanity. In turn, her warm compassionate gaze that wraps like a blanket around the infinitely bleak and shabby lives of her characters is the spark, the warmth of hope that the author delivers to her readers.

Pak Hye-kyung

양귀자

작가 양귀자는 1955년 전라북도 전주에서 5남 2녀 중 다섯 오빠 밑의 첫 딸로 태어났다. 1960년에 아버지가 사망하고, 큰오빠가 대가족의 생계를 꾸려 나가기 시작한다. 이러한 큰오빠의 헌신에 대한 작가 자신의 부채감은 후일 작품에서 투영되기도 한다. 1967년에 중학교에 입학한 뒤에는 도서관에서 살다시피 하며 소설 읽기에 탐닉한다. 1970년에 고등학교에 입학하면서 각종 백일장과 문예현상공모에 참가하기 시작했고, 본격적으로 소설 습작을 시작한다. 이어 1974년에 원광대학교 국어국문학과에 문예장학생으로 입학한다. 1978년에 원광대학교를 졸업한 뒤 청주시 호남고등학교에 국어 교사로 부임했다가 한 달 뒤 사퇴하고, 단지 섬이라는 이유만으로 전남 고흥군 거금도의 금상동중학교로 자원해 간다. 그리고 이해 5월 문예지 《문학사상》 신인상에 응모한 단편 「다시 시작하는 아침」과 「이미 닫힌 문」이 당선되면서 문단에 데뷔한다. 1980년에 교직을 사임하고 결혼하여 서울로 거처를 옮긴다.

Yang Kwi-ja

Yang Kwi-ja was born as the first daughter with five elder brothers, out of seven siblings in Chŏnju, Chŏllabuk-do, in 1955. After her father's death in 1955, her eldest brother became the head of the household, responsible for his large family's livelihood. The author feels tremendously indebted to her eldest brother for his dedication to, and sacrifice for, his family, and this sense of debt was later reflected in her work. After entering middle school in 1967, Yang was almost addicted to reading novels in the library, where she stayed all day. In 1970 she entered high school and began writing practice pieces and submitted an entry for various writing contests. In 1974, she entered the Department of Korean Language and Literature at Wonkwang University as a creative writing scholarship student. After graduating from college in 1978, she was assigned to teach Korean at Honam High School in Ch'ŏngju. She resigned from this post in a month and volunteered to teach at Kumsangdong Middle

1981년 이래 부천의 변두리 지역인 원미동에 거처하면서 단편을 집중적으로 써 내어 1985년에 첫 번째 소설집을 출간하고, 1987년에는 연작소설집 『원미동 사람들』을 출간한다. 『원미동 사람들』이 큰 호평을 받으면서 80년대를 대표하는 작가 중의 한 사람으로 자리매김 된다. 이어서 「천마총 가는 길」(1988), 「슬픔도 힘이 된다」(1990) 등의 대표작들을 연이어 발표한다. 장편 『나는 소망한다 내게 금지된 것을』(1992)이 출간되어 페미니즘 논쟁을 불러일으켰고, 영화로도 만들어진다. 같은 해에 발표한 중편 「숨은 꽃」으로 제16회 이상문학상을 수상한다. 1993년에 세 번째 작품집 『슬픔도 힘이 된다』를 묶어 낸다.

이후에는 중단편보다는 장편 창작에 몰두하게 된다. 현실의 변화에 걸맞은 작가 의식의 변화가 필요함을 강조하면서 독자와의 직접적인 의사소통을 주장한다. 1995년에 발표한 『천년의 사랑』이 공전의 베스트셀러가 된다. 이후 장편 『모순』(1998)을 출간하여 또 한 번 큰 성공을 거둔다.

School in Kogum Island, Kohŭng-gun, Chŏllanam-do, simply because the school was located in a remote island. She made her literary debut in May the same year, by winning the *Munhak Sasang* New Writer Award with short stories, "Morning of a New Beginning" and "Door Already Closed." In 1980, after her marriage, she resigned from her school and moved to Seoul.

Living in Wŏnmi-dong in the outskirt of Puch'ŏn since 1981, Yang published her first collection of short stories in 1985 and then a collection of a series of short stories entitled *Wŏnmi-dong People.* This latter collection was well received critically, and Yang was catapulted to fame, becoming one of the most representative writers of the 1980's. In the same period she published some of her most important short stories including "Road to Ch'ŏnmach'ong" (1988) and "Sadness Can Also Be Encouraging." (1990) In 1992, she published *I Desire What's Forbidden to Me*, a novel that caused controversy among feminist circles and was made a film. She won the Yi Sang Literary Award the same year for her novella "Hidden Flower." In 1993, she published her third collection of short stories, *Sadness Can Also Be Encouraging.*

Afterwards, she focused more on writing novels than short stories or novellas. She emphasizes the importance of a writer's transformation corresponding to changing reality and argues that a writer always needs to directly communicate with her readers. Her novel *Millennial Love* (1995) was a record bestseller. Her next novel *Contradiction* (1998) was also very popular among readers.

번역 **전미세리** Translated by Jeon Miseli

한국외국어대학교 동시통역대학원을 졸업한 후, 캐나다 브리티시컬럼비아 대학 도서관학, 아시아학과 문학 석사, 동 대학 비교문학과 박사 학위를 취득하고 강사 및 아시아 도서관 사서로 근무했다. 한국국제교류재단 장학금을 지원받았고, 캐나다 연방정부 사회인문과학연구회의 연구비를 지원받았다. 오정희의 단편 「직녀」를 번역했으며 그 밖에 서평, 논문 등을 출판했다.

Jeon Miseli is graduate from the Graduate School of Simultaneous Interpretation, Hankuk University of Foreign Studies and received her M.L.S. (School of Library and Archival Science), M.A. (Dept. of Asian Studies) and Ph.D. (Programme of Comparative Literature) at the University of British Columbia, Canada. She taught as an instructor in the Dept. of Asian Studies and worked as a reference librarian at the Asian Library, UBC. She was awarded the Korea Foundation Scholarship for Graduate Students in 2000. Her publications include the translation "Weaver Woman" (*Acta Koreana*, Vol. 6, No. 2, July 2003) from the original short story "Chingnyeo" (1970) written by Oh Jung-hee.

감수 K. E. 더핀 Edited by K. E. Duffin

시인, 화가, 판화가. 하버드 인문대학원 글쓰기 지도 강사를 역임하고, 현재 프리랜서 에디터, 글쓰기 컨설턴트로 활동하고 있다.

K. E. Duffin is a poet, painter and printmaker. She is currently working as a freelance editor and writing consultant as well. She was a writing tutor for the Graduate School of Arts and Sciences, Harvard University.

감수 **전승희** Edited by Jeon Seung-hee

번역문학가, 문학평론가. 하버드대학교 한국학연구소 연구원으로 재직 중이며 바흐친의 『장편소설과 민중언어』, 제인 오스틴의 『오만과 편견』 등을 공역했다.

Jeon Seung-hee is a literary critic and translator. She is currently a fellow at the Korea Institute, Harvard University. Her translations include Mikhail Bakhtin's *Novel and the People's Culture* and Jane Austen's *Pride and Prejudice*.

바이링궐 에디션 한국 현대 소설 010

원미동 시인

2012년 7월 25일 초판 1쇄 발행
2024년 5월 17일 초판 4쇄 발행

지은이 양귀자 | **옮긴이** 전미세리 | **펴낸이** 김재범
감수 K. E. Duffin, Jeon Seung-hee | **기획** 전성태, 정은경, 이경재
편집 정수인, 김형욱, 윤단비 | **관리** 박신영
펴낸곳 ㈜아시아 | **출판등록** 2006년 1월 27일 제406-2006-000004호
주소 경기도 파주시 회동길 445(서울 사무소: 서울특별시 동작구 서달로 161-1, 3층)
전화 02.3280.5058 | **팩스** 070.7611.2505 | **홈페이지** www.bookasia.org
ISBN 978-89-94006-20-8 (set) | 978-89-94006-29-1 (04810)
값은 뒤표지에 있습니다.

Bi-lingual Edition Modern Korean Literature 010

The Poet of Wŏnmi-dong

Written by Yang Kwi-ja | **Translated by** Jeon Miseli
Published by Asia Publishers
Address 445, Hoedong-gil, Paju-si, Gyeonggi-do, Korea
(Seoul Office:161-1, Seodal-ro, Dongjak-gu, Seoul, Korea)
Homepage Address www.bookasia.org | **Tel.** (822).3280.5058 | **Fax.** 070.7611.2505
First published in Korea by Asia Publishers 2012
ISBN 978-89-94006-20-8 (set) | 978-89-94006-29-1 (04810)

K-픽션 시리즈 | Korean Fiction Series

〈K-픽션〉 시리즈는 한국문학의 젊은 상상력입니다. 최근 발표된 가장 우수하고 흥미로운 작품을 엄선하여 출간하는 〈K-픽션〉은 한국문학의 생생한 현장을 국내외 독자들과 실시간으로 공유하고자 기획되었습니다. 〈바이링궐 에디션 한국 대표 소설〉 시리즈를 통해 검증된 탁월한 번역진이 참여하여 원작의 재미와 품격을 최대한 살린 〈K-픽션〉 시리즈는 매 계절마다 새로운 작품을 선보입니다.

001 버핏과의 저녁 식사-**박민규** Dinner with Buffett-**Park Min-gyu**
002 아르판-**박형서** Arpan-**Park hyoung su**
003 애드벌룬-**손보미** Hot Air Balloon-**Son Bo-mi**
004 나의 클린트 이스트우드-**오한기** My Clint Eastwood-**Oh Han-ki**
005 이베리아의 전갈-**최민우** Dishonored-**Choi Min-woo**
006 양의 미래-**황정은** Kong's Garden-**Hwang Jung-eun**
007 대니-**윤이형** Danny-**Yun I-hyeong**
008 퇴근-**천명관** Homecoming-**Cheon Myeong-kwan**
009 옥화-**금희** Ok-hwa-**Geum Hee**
010 시차-**백수린** Time Difference-**Baik Sou linne**
011 올드 맨 리버-**이장욱** Old Man River-**Lee Jang-wook**
012 권순찬과 착한 사람들-**이기호** Kwon Sun-chan and Nice People-**Lee Ki-ho**
013 알바생 자르기-**장강명** Fired-**Chang Kang-myoung**
014 어디로 가고 싶으신가요-**김애란** Where Would You Like To Go?-**Kim Ae-ran**
015 세상에서 가장 비싼 소설-**김민정** The World's Most Expensive Novel-**Kim Min-jung**
016 체스의 모든 것-**김금희** Everything About Chess-**Kim Keum-hee**
017 할로윈-**정한아** Halloween-**Chung Han-ah**
018 그 여름-**최은영** The Summer-**Choi Eunyoung**
019 어느 피씨주의자의 종생기-**구병모** The Story of P.C.-**Gu Byeong-mo**
020 모르는 영역-**권여선** An Unknown Realm-**Kwon Yeo-sun**
021 4월의 눈-**손원평** April Snow-**Sohn Won-pyung**
022 서우-**강화길** Seo-u-**Kang Hwa-gil**
023 가출-**조남주** Run Away-**Cho Nam-joo**
024 연애의 감정학-**백영옥** How to Break Up Like a Winner-**Baek Young-ok**
025 창모-**우다영** Chang-mo-**Woo Da-young**
026 검은 방-**정지아** The Black Room-**Jeong Ji-a**
027 도쿄의 마야-**장류진** Maya in Tokyo-**Jang Ryu-jin**
028 홀리데이 홈-**편혜영** Holiday Home-**Pyun Hye-young**
029 해피 투게더-**서장원** Happy Together-**Seo Jang-won**
030 골드러시-**서수진** Gold Rush-**Seo Su-jin**
031 당신이 보고 싶어하는 세상-**장강명** The World You Want to See-**Chang Kang-myoung**
032 지난밤 내 꿈에-**정한아** Last Night, In My Dream-**Chung Han-ah**
Special 휴가중인 시체-**김중혁** Corpse on Vacation-**Kim Jung-hyuk**
Special 사파에서-**방현석** Love in Sa Pa-**Bang Hyeon-seok**

K-포엣 시리즈 | Korean Poet Series

030 앙코르-**신동옥** Encore-**Shin Dong-ok**

029 내가 가진 산책길을 다 줄게-**정우신**
I'll Give You All My Promenade-**Jeong Woo-shin**

028 글자만 남은 아침-**박장호** A Morning with only Writing Left-**Park Jang-ho**

027 거의 모든 기쁨-**이소연** Nearly All Happiness-**Lee Soyoun**

026 설운 일 덜 생각하고-**문동만** Thinking Less about Sad Things-**Moon Dong-man**

025 새를 따라서-**박철** Following Birds-**Park Cheol**

024 여기까지가 미래입니다-**황인찬**
You Have Reached the End of the Future-**Hwang Inchan**

023 비물질-**이현호** Non-matter-**Lee hyun-ho**

022 굴 소년들-**이설야** Cave Boys-**Lee Sul-ya**

021 끝을 시작하기-**김 근** Beginning the End-**Kim Keun**

020 호랑나비-**황규관** Tiger Swallowtail-**Hwang Gyu-gwan**

019 자살충-**김성규** Suicide Parasite-**Kim Seong-gyu**

018 호모 마스크스-**김수열** Homo Maskus-**Kim Soo-yeol**

017 해저의 교실에서 소년은 흰 달을 본다-**장이지**
A Boy Is Looking at the White Moon from a Classroom Under the Sea-**Jang I-ji**

016 느낌은 멈추지 않는다-**안주철** Feeling Never Stops-**Ahn Joo-cheol**

015 해피랜드-**김해자** HappyLand-**Kim Hae-ja**

014 마트료시카 시침핀 연구회-**유형진**
The Society for Studies in Matryoshka and Basting Pins-**Yu Hyoung-jin**

013 여름만 있는 계절에 네가 왔다-**이영주**
You Arrived in the Season of Perennial Summer-**Lee Young-ju**

012 세계의 끝에서 우리는-**양안다** We, At the End of the World-**Yang Anda**

011 깊은 일-**안현미** Deep Work-**An Hyeon-mi**

010 해를 오래 바라보았다-**이영광** I Gave the Sun a Long Look-**Lee Young-kwang**

009 유령시인-**김중일** A Ghost Poet-**Kim Joong-il**

008 자수견본집-**김정환** An Embroidery Sampler-**Kim Jung-whan**

007 저녁의 고래-**정일근** Evening of the Whale-**Chung Il-keun**

006 **김현 시선 Poems by Kim Hyun**

005 **안상학 시선 Poems by Ahn Sang-Hak**

004 **허수경 시선 Poems by Huh Sukyung**

003 **백석 시선 Poems by Baek Seok**

002 **안도현 시선 Poems by Ahn Do-Hyun**